"This book starts on a fast pace and never slows down."
—Mary Gramlich, *The Reading Reviewer*

"Her Lords of Vice definitely live up to their names."
—Limecello

After Dark with a Scoundrel

"I absolutely loved *After Dark with a Scoundrel*. It is an amazing read and I could not put it down . . . I can't wait for the other Lords of Vice." —*Night Owl Romance*

"Those sexy Lords of Vice return as another member is caught in a maze of love and danger. Hawkins's talents for perfectly merging gothic elements into sexually charged romance are showcased along with the marvelous cast of characters taking readers on a thrill ride." —*Romantic Times BOOKreviews* (4 stars)

"A 'must-read' . . . *After Dark with a Scoundrel* is a fast-paced Regency historical romance with a new and exciting surprise just about every time you turn a page . . . as stunning as it is riveting. This story has it all . . . scorching." —*Romance Junkies Reviews*

"The sparks between Regan and Dare are beautifully written, so that you can almost feel them coming off the pages." —*Book Reading Gals*

"4½ stars. The intensity between Regan and Dare sizzles on the pages." —*Romance Dish*

"Ms. Hawkins knows just how to pull the best from her characters to make you care for them, love them, get irritated with them, and all those other delicious emotions we romance readers need in our books."

—*The Good, The Bad, and The Unread* (A+)

"Perfect explosion of emotional fireworks blasted off the pages and set the rest of the tone for the book."

—*Romantic Crush Junkies* (4.5 quills)

"Poignant, sweetly romantic and sexy as can be."

—*Reader to Reader*

Till Dawn with the Devil

"*Till Dawn with the Devil*'s romance is first-rate with unusual characters and an underlying mystery that will intrigue readers." —Robin Lee, *Romance Reviews Today*

"A terrific second book in this series. I had it read in a day and then bemoaned the fact it was over."

—*The Good, The Bad, and The Unread* (A+)

"You will devour every sexy and intriguing morsel of this divine read." —*Romantic Crush Junkies* (4 stars)

"Hawkins cements her reputation for bringing compelling, unique, and lush romances to fans eager for fresh storytelling." —*Romantic Times BOOKreviews* (4 stars)

"Delightful and enjoyed every delicious minute of the book." —*Single Titles* (5 stars)

Also by
ALEXANDRA HAWKINS

All Afternoon with a Scandalous Marquess

Sunrise with a Notorious Lord

After Dark with a Scoundrel

Till Dawn with the Devil

All Night with a Rogue

Dusk
with a
Dangerous
Duke

Alexandra Hawkins

St. Martin's Paperbacks

This is a work of fiction. All of the characters, organizations, and events portrayed in this novel are either products of the author's imagination or are used fictitiously.

DUSK WITH A DANGEROUS DUKE

Copyright © 2013 by Alexandra Hawkins.

For information address St. Martin's Press, 175 Fifth Avenue, New York, NY 10010.

ISBN: 978-1-250-00138-2

Printed in the United States of America

St. Martin's Paperbacks edition / March 2013

St. Martin's Paperbacks are published by St. Martin's Press, 175 Fifth Avenue, New York, NY 10010.

10 9 8 7 6 5 4 3 2 1

"Vices are their own punishment."
—Aesop

Prologue

"Nicolas, there you are." His grandmother's sharp gaze settled on him as she beckoned impatiently for him to enter. "Come . . . join us. You may remain, young Vanewright, if you are able to refrain from disrupting our meeting."

"Thank you, madam," Christopher blurted out automatically, and then winced when Nicolas's grandmother and her male companions halted their discussion and stared at him. His friend shrugged sheepishly. "My apologies. It won't happen again—madam."

Nicolas Stuart Towers, Duke of Huntsley, gave his friend a pitying look. He had stood silently on numerous occasions as his grandmother had reduced grown men to quivering, spineless specimens with a stern look. It was no surprise that his twelve-year-old companion was terrified of the wizened old dragon.

In truth, even he was a little frightened of her.

After he'd lost both of his parents to influenza six

years earlier, his grandmother had come to live with him at Telcliff Castle. She had told the grieving Nicolas that he needed a strong hand and guidance now that he had inherited the dukedom, and the dowager was capable of delivering both. Not counting some distant cousins, his grandmother was the only family that he had left. She was a tough old bird, but he loved her dearly. There was nothing he would not do for her.

Assuming Christopher would keep a respectful distance, Nicolas headed toward his grandmother and her companions. As he crossed the room, his gaze was drawn to one of the corners where a small child was inconsolably weeping. Even with her ruddy cheeks blotchy with tears, she was a pretty little thing with her mop of blond curls and a mutinous pout on her bow-shaped mouth. His smooth brow furrowed with mild curiosity as he observed a harried nursemaid wrap her arms around the two-year-old while uttering hushed, unintelligible assurances.

Dismissing the unknown girl from his thoughts, he politely bowed to his grandmother and the two gentlemen. The man to her left was his grandmother's solicitor, Mr. Porter. The other gentleman was a stranger.

"Grandmother, I was unaware that we had guests this afternoon."

The child in the corner howled her indignation.

The dowager's left eyelid twitched and her mouth tightened with disapproval, but she did not glance in the girl's direction. This was extraordinary, since his grandmother had patience neither for disruptions nor for the little girls who caused them. Instead, she placed her hand on Nicolas's back and gently nudged him to join the two men.

"Nicolas, you are acquainted with Mr. Porter. Allow me to introduce you to an old and dear friend of mine, Sir Auden Castell."

Nicolas bowed. "Good afternoon, sir."

Sir Auden appeared to be as ancient as his grandmother. In his youth, he must have cut an impressive figure with his height and girth. However, time had not been kind to the elderly gentleman. His shoulders had bowed with age, giving him a sizable hump on his upper back. What muscle he possessed had withered and turned to fat, but his brown eyes were friendly as they assessed Nicolas from head to toe.

"Mary, you have a fine lad squiring you about these days," Sir Auden said, his baritone voice warm with approval.

Mary, Nicolas thought, his dark eyebrows shooting upward in curiosity. The gentleman was a very good friend of his grandmother's to be bandying about her given name so freely.

Not that his grandmother needed his protection. With the loss of her husband and her son, she had made a place for herself in a social world that was dominated by her male peers. The respect she commanded was to be envied and admired, and he was confident that gentlemen would see him in the same manner.

His grandmother accepted Sir Auden's compliment with a nod of her head. "It was a tragedy that Nicolas has been deprived of my son's guidance. Nevertheless, he is a Towers. The strength of his bloodline guides him instinctively. He was born with the honor and compassion to be a protector of his people, and I have come to depend on my grandson in all matters."

Nicolas stood silently, a slightly dazed expression on his face. He felt as if his grandmother had cuffed him hard on the skull instead of offering praise. The dowager did not believe in false praise or coddling. In her opinion, it fostered weakness, which explained why there were always a few males in every generation who were incapable of living up to the Towers name. She certainly would not tolerate such flaws in her only grandson, who had a duty not only to the family name but also to the people who depended on him.

After the loss of his parents, the dowager's approval meant everything to him. His narrow chest puffed with pride with the knowledge his grandmother held him in such high esteem.

"I am satisfied," Sir Auden said to the dowager. "Porter, is the paperwork in order so we can make it official?"

Mr. Porter gave the spectacles sliding down his nose an absent push before he gathered up the papers on his desk. "I will need both you and Her

Grace to review what I've prepared, but I believe you will be pleased."

"Excellent," Sir Auden said, clapping the solicitor on the shoulder. "Good work, Porter. I knew we could count on you."

"Yes, well done, Samuel," the dowager concurred. "Your discretion regarding our delicate situation is appreciated."

"What is going on, Grandmother?" Nicolas politely interjected.

Sir Auden blinked in surprise. "Have you not told him?"

The dowager drew herself up at the mild rebuke. "There was no point in involving the boy until we had come to an agreement and all parties were present."

"Tell me what precisely?"

She glanced impatiently at him, for it was uncommon for him or anyone else to interrupt her. "Your marriage to Lady Grace Kearly. It is an excellent match. Your bride is the daughter of a duke and possesses an exceptional dowry. Her pure lineage and wealth will be an asset to the family. I hope you appreciate your good fortune."

Good fortune? Nicolas could not form a proper response to the outrageous statement. He was too young to marry. What about his education? And his private thoughts of traveling the world? Hell, he had yet to bed his first female!

Out of desperation, he looked to Christopher for

silent support. His friend was the Earl of Vane-wright, and as far as Nicolas knew *his* family was not trying to marry him off before he grew his first beard. Unfortunately, Christopher was blithely oblivious to his friend's plight. At some point, he had wandered over to the pretty nursemaid and her young charge. The little girl was sitting contently on Christopher's hip while he flirted with the servant.

What a fine friend he was, Nicolas thought. He was in trouble and Christopher was chasing after a bit of skirt who was never going to let herself be caught.

"Nicolas, did you hear a single word I've uttered?"

He swallowed thickly and shook his head. His skull felt like it was stuffed with straw; worse, he worried that he might disgrace himself and faint.

"I'm too young to marry."

His soft admission earned a few sympathetic chuckles from Mr. Porter and Sir Auden. The dowager, on the other hand, had pursed her lips together, a visible sign of her displeasure.

"Who said anything of you marrying this very day?" she snapped, and for Nicolas, it might as well have been a lash. "These arrangements are often set in place years before the actual marriage takes place. I thought you would be more grateful."

"I am, Grandmother," he mumbled, not feeling appreciative at all. He was old enough to know that money and beauty did not always go hand in hand. What if he had to marry a lady so long in the tooth that no man would have her?

"So I can see," the dowager replied.

Too vexed to speak further on the subject, she beckoned for his friend to join them. She was probably going to banish him and Christopher from her sight. They would be lucky to get supper this evening.

Still holding the two-year-old girl, his friend crossed the room with the nursemaid following in his wake. "How may I be of service, Your Grace?"

Braggart, Nicolas thought uncharitably.

"Such a pretty child," his grandmother said, opening her arms. "I believe she likes you, Vanewright."

"I suppose," Christopher replied cautiously as he finally sensed the tension pouring off his friend.

"Give her to me."

"Of course, Your Grace." He took a step forward and handed the girl to the dowager.

His grandmother smiled at the child. She cast a shrewd glance at her grandson. "Your parents' early deaths deprived you of siblings, Nicolas. Come . . . why do you not hold her a moment."

Considering the amount of trouble he was in, Nicolas immediately held out his hands and accepted the light burden even though he had no interest in the child. His thoughts were on bigger problems. Unused to handling young children, he felt awkward and the two-year-old seemed to sense his discomfort. She immediately reached out for Christopher and made soft anxious sounds.

Rebuffed by a sniveling girl. Nicolas doubted his afternoon could get worse.

"She's as twitchy as a monkey," Nicolas said with false cheer, struggling not to drop her as she tried to free herself from his grasp. "Does she have a name?"

"Of course," his grandmother said drily. "Lady Grace Kearly."

The girl slipped through his boneless grasp, her backside hitting the floor first. Everyone in the room gasped. Lady Grace promptly let out an earsplitting scream.

"It was an accident!" he hastily explained to the scowling adults.

Horrified that he might have hurt the child, Nicolas fell to his knees and wrapped his arms around her with the intention of collecting her off the floor. This—girl—was his bride? Was this some kind of jest?

Frustrated and in no mood to be handled, the girl leaned forward and sank her teeth into his wrist. Nicolas yelped in pain. Those tiny sharp teeth sliced into his flesh and drew blood.

Evidently, Lady Grace didn't think much of their arranged marriage, either.

Chapter One

February 2, 1825, near Frethwell Hall

It was a cold bitter night for traveling the rough northern countryside roads on horseback. Stubborn and foolhardy, Hunter silently acknowledged his current predicament as he thought of the dry, comfortable coach he had abandoned at the last inn three hours behind him. Warm and his belly full, his coachman was likely savoring his fifth pot of ale in front of the hearth as he regaled his companions with raunchy tales of his master's exploits and the madness that had burned in his brain like a fever.

Not madness, Hunter amended.

Fate.

And the lady had a name—Lady Grace Kearly.

She was the reason he and his horse were tearing up miles of road on this godforsaken night. He had fought this inevitable meeting for too many years, but he had run out of time.

It was time to collect his unwanted bride.

I should have visited Frethwell Hall two years ago when Porter urged me to set aside the time.

Not that Hunter hadn't tried to rectify his mistake.

In the past nine months, he had tried to visit Lady Grace. Twice. Both times he had been turned away. The butler had told him that his mistress was not in residence. She had been away visiting friends, and no one seemed to know when she would return.

At the time, a part of him had been relieved by his unexpected reprieves. However, time was running out for both him and Lady Grace, and his impulsive visit to Frethwell Hall this evening was bound to delay his return to London.

You had nineteen years to collect her, gent.

Hunter shook off the twinge of regret before it took hold of him. Besides, anger was more palatable. In truth, he had his grandmother to thank for his lamentable circumstances. If the wily old woman had not died when he was still young enough to be intimidated by her, he might have been able to talk his way out of this arranged marriage.

His horse squealed as Hunter abruptly tugged on the reins to bring the animal to a halt. Annoyed with his rider's rough treatment, the horse snorted and shook his head while Hunter squinted at the lights in the distance.

He absently leaned forward and patted the horse's thick-muscled neck. "There, there . . . Draw comfort in knowing that your misery is almost over, whilst mine is just beginning."

Lady Grace awaited the prize his grandmother had promised her grandfather.

She would soon be the Duchess of Huntsley.

"I'll wager she has teeth that'll remind me of a mare and hair thick and coarse like thatching," Hunter said, glaring at the country house in the distance. "Not to mention, a nasty disposition and voice that suits a sailor rather than a duchess."

His solicitor, however, would vehemently disagree with Hunter's description. According to Porter, Lady Grace possessed a beauty that would inspire artists, a voice that made angels weep with envy, and a sweet disposition.

Ha! Porter was capable of lying to gain Hunter's cooperation. The old scar on his wrist and the young lady's elusiveness proved that the hoyden still lurked beneath the social polish and instruction that she had received over the years.

A cold drop of rain struck him on cheek, causing him to glance heavenward. He was going to be soaked if he tarried. It was just one more thing that he could blame Lady Grace for since she had first announced to a dismayed Porter a year and a half ago that she was beginning to have second thoughts about the marriage contract struck when they were children. Porter's visit with the stubborn wench last month had proven Lady Grace's opinion on the subject had not improved.

Well, it was up to Hunter to change her mind.

With a wordless shout, he spurred the weary animal toward the distant lights.

As Hunter had predicted, the rain was almost blinding by the time he had reached the house. Cold, hungry, and too angry to be civil company for anyone, he tethered the horse and strode to the front door with an impatient stride. He pounded his fist against the solid oak surface and was forced to wait five minutes before his knocks roused someone's curiosity.

A thin, middle-aged man opened the door wide enough to poke his head and a small lantern through the opening. Hunter recognized the man as Lady Grace's butler.

"'Tis a foul night for a man to be out on the roads."

"No truer words have been spoken, my good man," Hunter said, striving for a civil tone. If he could not get past Lady Grace's gatekeeper, then he would have no success with the mistress of Frethwell Hall. "My apologies for interrupting your supper. Due to this abominable weather, the journey took longer than expected."

Obviously deducing from Hunter's speech that his unexpected visitor was a nobleman, the servant straightened and opened the door wider. "There's no reason why you should tarry in the rain. Come into the hall, Your Grace."

So the man recognized him. This was an unexpected boon. Hunter was happy to oblige. "Ah, good! Then you know who I am."

"Your disappointment at our last meeting made an impression."

Belatedly, he recalled his tired, wet horse and grimaced. "My horse will need attending as well."

The butler's brows lifted in surprise as he peered outside. "You were not traveling by coach?"

Hunter chuckled, "Only a madman would brave such weather on horseback, eh?"

His coachman had said as much to his face.

"Or a man in love," the servant replied while he shut the door, missing his companion's look of astonishment. "However, I suspect you have not succumbed to either affliction."

"How can you tell?"

"Simple enough, I suppose. My job requires me to take a swift measure of a man's character," the butler said casually as he walked by Hunter to set the oil lamp on a narrow table. "I wouldn't be protecting my mistress if I opened the door to just anyone who wandered down the gravel road, now would I?"

With admirable efficiency, the butler stripped Hunter of his greatcoat and hat. "Stay here. You're making a fine mess on the floor, and I'd rather mop up one large puddle instead of a dozen smaller ones. I'll get you a blanket and summon one of the boys to see to your horse. Then we'll see about getting you dry, and, if you have the inclination, something to warm your belly."

"Wait!" Hunter called out. "Before you see to the blanket, you might want to let your mistress know of my arrival."

"It is unnecessary, Your Grace."

Hunter knew he wasn't a madman, but he was beginning to wonder about Lady Grace's butler. "Why? Is she hiding in the shadows overhead?"

The butler paused, and gave him a shrewd glance. "My lady is not a spiritless creature, Your Grace. You will not find her lurking in the corners."

He was in no mood to listen to the servant's defense of his mistress. "Then where is she? Speak plainly because I am too cold and wet for civility."

The butler gave him a hesitant look. "I cannot say, Your Grace. My lady departed Frethwell Hall more than a fortnight past."

Hunter brought his hand to his face and noted that his fingers trembled. He preferred to blame the weariness creeping into his bones, but he was only fooling himself.

He was bloody furious.

The woman was going to be the death of him. He had traveled all this way for *nothing*. Porter had once told him that the blasted woman rarely traveled beyond her parish. It had taken Hunter nineteen years to come up to scratch. The least the woman could do was remain at home so he could formally declare his intentions.

"Where is she?" he demanded.

Loyalty to his lady warred with self-preservation. "Your Grace—"

Hunter marched up to the servant.

"N-north," the man blurted out before Hunter could throttle the answer out of him. "I heard she journeyed north to visit a sick friend."

"Of course she isn't here," he said, mostly to himself. "The one place she should be."

"And why is that, if you don't mind me asking?" the butler asked.

"Because I am here!" Hunter replied, thumping his fist on his chest with frustration, "—in the middle of nowhere." Cold, wet, and hungry. "While your lady is savoring a warm hearth and the company of her good friend. I must confess—what the devil is your name?"

"Copper, sir," the butler helpfully supplied.

"Well, Copper, I must confess that it is becoming apparent that your mistress is proving to be difficult. It is an unpleasant trait for a wife."

Perhaps it was unfair to judge the absent lady so harshly, but he was not in a reasonable mood.

"Quite right." The butler cleared his throat. "Though perhaps you are mistaken about the lady's intentions?"

"I highly doubt it."

How many times had Porter chastised Hunter about his lack of interest in joining him on his annual visit to Frethwell Hall? His solicitor and his future bride failed to appreciate the demands on his time. Without a doubt, his absence had provoked Lady Grace's defiance, and Porter had washed his hands of the entire affair. The elderly man even had the audacity to order Hunter to rectify the situation.

It was the reason why he was there on such a god-forsaken night.

Hunter's eyes narrowed on the butler. "Copper, are you aware that your mistress has ignored my missives?"

He had sent three. The last one had been sent after Porter's visit. However, the lady had failed to respond.

The butler hastily glanced away. "It is not my place to speculate, Your Grace."

"Your lady is vexed with my behavior," he said, already guessing the butler's response. "Porter has said as much on numerous occasions."

"Please, Your Grace," the butler entreated. "I have been with the little mistress since she was a child, and I would not wish for her to view me in an unfavorable light."

Was Lady Grace intending to alter her fate?

It was a tempting thought. One he had pondered over the years when deep in his cups. Perhaps they had more in common that he thought.

The butler's loyalty to Lady Grace should have annoyed Hunter, but he tilted his head back and laughed. "I doubt there is a gentleman who is more deserving of your lady's ire than I."

The declaration was supposed to cheer the old servant. Instead the man looked utterly grim. "Give me time and I might be able to come up with another name or two."

Nineteen years was a long time for a bride to wait.

Hunter offered no apology, but he was not blind to his many sins.

In a friendly gesture, he clapped the butler on the back. "Care to wager on it, my good fellow?"

Chapter Two

March 13, 1825, Frethwell Hall

"Straightaway, I knew the starlings were a sign of things to come."

Grace glanced up from her book and turned her attention to her agitated servant. "What starlings?"

Rosemary plucked the book from her mistress's hands and placed it on the table. "He insists on seeing you at once. 'Tis a shame there is no time to change your dress. This one is heading for the rag bin, but it will have to do."

Concerned, Grace stood and stilled the housekeeper's attempts to tidy the library. "Slow down. What about the starlings?"

The servant closed her eyes and murmured a soft prayer. When she opened her eyes, the stark worry in her gaze made Grace's stomach flutter. "Dead. Fifty of them. They fell out of the sky and hit the front lawn like black stones. Their wings and heads were twisted at horrible angles."

Grace brought her fingers to her lips. "Good grief! When did this happen? No one said a word of it."

"That was my doing," Rosemary explained. "I did not want to frighten you. But it's a dark omen to be certain. His Grace's arrival is proof enough."

Her breath caught in her throat. *He* was here. Her wait was finally over. "I do not believe it. Are you telling me that the Duke of Huntsley has arrived?"

She glanced down at her plain dress in alarm. Rosemary was correct. Her dress was entirely unsuitable for her first meeting with the gentleman she was betrothed to marry.

Grace frowned. Well, second meeting, she silently amended. She had been too young to recall the occasion. "I cannot have him see me in this dress."

"Not *that* duke," the older woman said, smoothing some of the wrinkles with her hand. "The other one. And there is no time to fret about your dress. I told him that you required a few minutes, but his sort do not like waiting for anyone. He will be here at any moment."

A polite knock heralded the arrival of her unexpected visitor.

Rosemary was all business when she strode across the room and opened the door. "Lady Grace will see you now," she said cheerfully, refraining from pointing out that the duke should have waited for the butler to bring him upstairs.

"Your Grace," Grace said. She was unable to match her housekeeper's false cheery demeanor, so she simply smiled as she curtsied. "What an unexpected pleasure."

Of course, she was lying.

There was very little Grace liked about her uncle.

The second son of the Duke and Duchess of Strangham, Lord Gasper had inherited the title from Grace's father at his unexpected death. According to her grandfather, her uncle had donned his mourning clothes as was expected, while he quietly started spending the family's fortune on horses, lavish parties, and mistresses. He might have exhausted Grace's inheritance as well if not for her grandfather's shrewd decision to betroth her to the young Duke of Huntsley.

As a child, she could recall the heated arguments between her grandfather and uncle. On numerous occasions, her grandfather had warned her to keep her distance from Strangham. He was not to be trusted, he had said. Unfortunately, her grandfather had passed away and could no longer protect her. The passing years had claimed the life of the dowager, too. As for the Duke of Huntsley, well, His Grace had more important business than visiting Frethwell Hall.

In his stead, she received an annual visit from the duke's solicitor Mr. Porter.

So she endured her uncle's visits, which were infrequent and blessedly brief. She could not fathom why he bothered to call on her. He did not seem to appreciate her or her home, Frethwell Hall.

After a brief hesitation, the Duke of Strangham clasped her hand, encouraging her to rise. "Good

afternoon, niece. How charming you look. Did I catch
you at some light housekeeping? I thought Huntsley
was taking better care of you than that."

Grace managed to keep her pleasant expression in
place, even though she longed to pick up the book
she had been reading and hurl it at the duke's head.
Her uncle always reminded her that the Duke of
Huntsley's protection was in name only.

"I confess, I was not prepared for visitors this afternoon, Uncle," she said, moving aside as he walked
to the center of the room. "As for the duke, do not
fret. I am provided with everything that I require."

Her uncle ran two fingers over one of the tables and
examined them. He made a soft disgruntled noise as
he rubbed the imaginary dust from his finger.

His eyebrows lifted as he glanced in her direction. "Ah, so you have heard from him recently."

Grace tried not to fidget under his scrutiny. "His
solicitor visited last month."

"You are referring to astute Mr. Porter, are you
not?"

The duke's tone implied that he did not think the
man was astute at all.

"Mr. Porter is fully capable of conveying my
wishes to the Duke of Huntsley. If you must know
the truth, I am quite spoiled by His Grace's generosity."

She wanted for nothing except the man himself.
In that instance, the duke was downright miserly,
giving everyone but her his personal attention.

Her uncle extended his hand, inviting her to join him on the sofa. "You are indeed fortunate, my dear."

She placed her hand on his and they sat down together.

"I heard gossip about Huntsley when I was in London last month."

"You surprise me, Uncle. I would not take you as one who would pay attention to such tripe."

His mouth thinned at her light rebuke, but it did not prevent him from sharing what he had heard. "Normally, I do not bother. However, I have discovered over the years that most of the gossip I have heard about Huntsley and his acquaintances is true. In fact, most of the stories are understated in a useless attempt to protect their families and the innocent who have the misfortune to be connected to these scurrilous gentlemen."

Grace looked down at her hands. She doubted her uncle's news about Huntsley was anything she wished to hear. She had deduced years ago that the gentleman took a perverse pleasure in sharing personal details about the duke that would inevitably hurt her feelings. She subtly straightened her posture and awaited the verbal blow.

"Your concern is touching, but unnecessary," she said, offering him a faint smile. "I may be sheltered here at Frethwell Hall, but the London gossip does make its way out to the country."

Any hope that her uncle would drop the subject was dashed at his next words. "I only intended to share good news. Rumor has it that Huntsley has parted ways with his latest mistress. Granted, these soiled doves only share his bed briefly, but this particular woman had managed to dig her tender hooks into the duke. Their arrangement lasted for several months, and the woman was quite devastated to lose such a flush protector."

Protector.

Grace had grown to despise the word. She wondered how many women the Duke of Huntsley had taken as mistresses over the years. Since the subject was viewed as inappropriate drawing room conversation, she was not well versed in the rules of engagement. For instance, how did one go about procuring a mistress? And once the gentleman tired of the relationship, how did he end it? Did the duke send Mr. Porter to deliver the unfortunate news to the poor woman?

Her silence seemed to please her uncle. He had come to stir the pot of mischief by revealing the sordid nature of her betrothed, and he had succeeded. Grace could have pinched herself for falling for her uncle's predictable ruse. She raised her chin and met his gaze to prove that his news had not upset her as he had hoped. When she was alone, she could allow herself to cry.

"Is it wrong for me to pity the scorned woman, Uncle?" she inquired. "A part of me does, though her loss was inevitable. As you know, my twenty-first birthday approaches, and the time has come for the

Duke of Huntsley to clean house if he plans on honoring the marriage pact his grandmother and my grandfather arranged."

For the first time, the Duke of Strangham struggled with his words. He had presented her with a clear case of the Duke of Huntsley's infidelity, and she, in turn, had praised the scoundrel for ending the affair.

"My dear, I do not believe you comprehend the man's true nature."

"Most brides do not," she said, her voice hardening ever so slightly. "Otherwise, we would not be so eager to legally bind ourselves to one man."

"And knowing this, you are still prepared to marry Huntsley?"

Grace shrugged. "An agreement was struck. I am prepared to see it through. Our family honor is at stake."

"What if I told you that I fear Huntsley has no intention of marrying you."

Nineteen years had passed since her marriage to the Duke of Huntsley had been arranged. As a child, the duke's absence had not troubled her, but the woman she had become understood the implications.

The duke rejected her as his duchess.

Once she had believed him to be a man of honor. However, she suspected a marriage born out of duty made for a cold marriage bed. Besides, the Duke of Huntsley's bed was filled with so many women, there was no room for her.

She kept her doubts to herself. To her uncle, she said, "Mr. Porter assured me that His Grace will return to Frethwell Hall before my birthday, and our marriage will take place. I assume it will be an intimate affair, but I pray you will attend."

"Damn Porter, and to Hades with Huntsley!"

Grace gasped in surprise as her uncle seized her by the shoulders. "Your Grace!"

"See here, girl," he said, his fingers digging into her flesh. "The Kearlys do not breed dimwits, and my encounters with you have revealed that you do possess an intellect higher than most ladies your age."

"Thank you—"

"Silence!" he shouted, and her eyes widened at his outburst. "I have tried to reason with kindness, but I see that I must be blunt. Huntsley will never marry you. His grandmother and your stubborn grandfather foisted you off on him because your impeccable bloodlines and wealth were considered an asset to the Towers family."

Her throat tightened as he gave her private fears a voice. "Nothing has changed."

Her uncle gave her an incredulous look. "Everything has changed. The dowager is dead, and Huntsley has no desire to take a bride—particularly one not of his own choosing. You must face the truth, my dear niece. Huntsley has abandoned you. Even now, he scours London for a new lady to fill his empty bed. Any lady will do as long as it is not you."

His words were so beyond cruel, Grace blindly

pushed her uncle aside and rose from the sofa. Was it all true? Had Mr. Porter been lying to her all of these long years so the duke had use of her fortune? What would happen to her once she turned twenty-one and the terms of the arranged marriage went unfulfilled?

"I see that I have distressed you." He stood and strode to her side. When he placed his hands on her, the touch was tender. "Forgive me, my child. It is a harsh truth to burden an innocent heart."

Still in denial, Grace shook her head. "I will write Mr. Porter. No . . . I will write the duke directly. I will demand an audience immediately."

"How many times have you written Huntsley over the years?" he gently countered. "How many times were you denied the courtesy of a reply?"

Too many.

Grace felt the brush of her uncle's fingers as he pressed a handkerchief into her hand. She silently cursed, realizing she had tears on her cheeks. "I am not crying," she muttered as she wiped away the wetness.

"Of course not, child."

She discreetly studied her uncle as she tended to her face. Although his voice and touch had been gentle, it was the fierce triumph in his eyes that troubled her. Her grandfather's warning that her uncle could not be trusted soothed her bruised heart.

"You are too kind, Uncle," she said, returning his handkerchief to him. "It dismays me to disagree with you, but I believe you are wrong about the Duke of Huntsley. He will come for me."

"And if you are wrong?"

"Then I will not marry him," she said simply. "I will be of age, and have control over my inheritance. London's polite society will eagerly embrace a titled heiress."

"Not precisely, dear niece." The Duke of Strangham's gaunt visage hardened, emphasizing the lines time had furrowed into his flesh. "If Huntsley fails to marry you by your twenty-first birthday, then your lands and investments are placed in my hands as your only living male relative."

She could not believe it. Why had no one told her?

Grace offered him a practiced smile. "I am no longer a child, Uncle. I can manage my own lands."

Her steward and Mr. Porter had been offering their guidance for years. There was no reason why they could not continue to do so.

"That is not how the courts will see it," he said pointedly. "If Huntsley cries off, you will no longer have the protection of the Towers name and influence. I am confident that the courts will see things my way. Besides, my brother would wish me to look after his daughter."

Grace felt cornered, but she managed not to react to her uncle's baiting. "I appreciate your generous offer. However, in the coming weeks you will see that your concern is unwarranted. The Duke of Huntsley will marry me."

Her uncle chuckled softly and shook his head. "Foolish child. Very well, we will see this through to its humiliating end. I will visit you again."

Grace turned away, avoiding the chaste kiss her uncle attempted to place on her cheek. "Good afternoon, Uncle. Shall I send you an invitation to the wedding?"

He gave her a pitying glance. "Huntsley is likely rutting between the fleshy thighs of his latest conquest, and you stand before me feathering your dreams with the misguided hope that the man possesses honor where you are concerned. I pray that you will be more sensible the next time we speak."

Grace sank into the nearest chair the moment the door closed. Before she could bring her hands to her face, the door opened again.

Rosemary rushed into the room. "Well, blessed be that His Grace has finally departed. This visit was longer than the other ones. I cannot fathom how you—" Finally noting Grace's blank expression, she put aside her diatribe on the Duke of Strangham. "You poor girl . . . what did your uncle say to you?"

One fact had become abundantly clear. The Duke of Huntsley could no longer protect her as her grandfather had intended. "Rosemary, tell the staff that preparations need to be made for a journey."

The older woman stared down at her. "Where?"

"London."

This time of year, it was perhaps unwise to visit the town while His Grace was in residence. Then again, it was the last place he would expect to find her.

The housekeeper's jaw slackened and then snapped shut. "I thought you were waiting for the Duke of Huntsley?"

Her eyes and nostrils flared at the notion. "I have already waited nineteen years for the man. I refuse to sit here another day. The Duke of Huntsley can go to perdition. I am going to London."

"But London. Why ever for?"

She recalled her uncle's confidence in securing her inheritance, which in turn would guarantee her compliance. "Why else would I travel to London? I intend to secure a husband."

And she knew just the lady who could assist her on her quest.

Chapter Three

Two weeks later, London

Grace refused to show up at Lady Netherley's door empty-handed, so she had ordered the coachman to halt at the first flower stall or cart that he came across. Her request had extended her drive through town, but she did not mind. The weather was temperate, and she suspected the marchioness would appreciate the thoughtful gesture.

Grace also hoped the flowers would soften Lady Netherley's disposition toward her since she was preparing to request a great boon from the lady.

The coachman found a stall not far from Covent Garden. While Grace longed to explore the market, this was not the day to do so. Another day, she promised herself. Rosemary would want to join her on such an outing as well.

"I could fetch yer posies if the sun is too strong for ye," the gruff coachman offered when he opened the door.

"I thank you for your offer, but I have my parasol," Grace said, though she made no attempt to open it.

Instead she accepted the coachman's hand as she stepped down from the coach. "I shall not be long."

Since she did not want to be late for her appointment, Grace came to a decision quickly, choosing lilacs and ferns for Lady Netherley. The delicate blooms rarely lasted beyond a day, but the fragrance always managed to cheer her.

"How much do I owe you?" she asked the girl who was wrapping her flowers in paper to keep them fresh.

"I have it," a deep masculine voice said beside her.

"A generous offer but unnecessary," Grace said, glancing over her shoulder but what she glimpsed froze her in place. Her startled gaze locked with warm, light brown eyes that reminded her of colored glass illuminated by the morning sun. There was humor and intelligence, and something she could not quite define in those beautiful depths as he leaned forward to pay the owner of the flower stall.

"Oh . . . I," she said, feeling flustered by his closeness so she focused on his dark coat sleeve as money exchanged hands.

Large hands, encased in expensive gloves. The fabric and precise fitting of his coat sleeves revealed wealth and a skilled tailor. Most impressive were the strong, muscular arms that filled out the fabric. Her mouth went dry at the thought of him turning, and those strong limbs wrapping around her, enfolding her in an embrace.

Her cheeks felt scalded by the unbidden desire to step closer and take scandalous liberties.

"A good afternoon to you both," the girl said, slipping the coins into a pocket as she placed the wrapped flowers into Grace's hands. With a distracted expression on her face, the girl turned to greet another patron, leaving Grace alone with the gentleman.

"Permit me to pay you for the flowers," Grace said, uncomfortable with her unexpected reaction to this man. Nor did she require his charity. Mr. Porter had told her often enough that she was an heiress. She could have bought the entire flower stall, if that had been her desire.

Desire. A troublesome word when this man was in her presence.

"I hate to deny a lady, but alas, I must refuse," was the man's cheerful reply.

Grace glanced up and noticed that she was not alone in her bemusement. With a brazenness that should have frightened her, the gentleman appeared to be taking the measure of her face. There was tenderness, longing, and even regret as he contemplated the delicate line of her nose, the shallow hollows of her cheeks, and the blush that most likely added a healthy glow to her cheeks.

He was truly the most handsome man Grace had ever encountered.

Her throat tightened with warring emotions.

The gentleman gestured toward the street. "Is that your coach?"

"Yes, it is."

Grace avoided meeting the stranger's gaze out of

fear that he might become emboldened by her interest. The instinctive gesture disconcerted her, causing her to freeze midstep. It was then that it occurred to her that she had spent most of her life discouraging her admirers because she was betrothed to the Duke of Huntsley.

It was a habit she intended to discard immediately.

Especially when staring at such a beautiful man gave her a sense of power and pleasure. She raised her chin, and was not surprised that her companion had no qualms when it came to staring at *her*. He had been patiently waiting for her to acknowledge him, and his polite smile widened into genuine delight that her admiration was undisguised.

Good grief, he was tall. And mightily handsome. From beneath the brim of his hat, those amazing light brown eyes shimmered and glinted like gold in the sunshine. His face was without blemish, but his strong features marked him as a seasoned gentleman. She doubted she had ever behaved so brazenly with a complete stranger, let alone a man.

"Will you permit me the pleasure of escorting you to your coach?"

Grace glanced in the direction of the coach, and she saw that the coachman had also noticed the stranger's open interest in his mistress. She shook her head, signaling to the servant that all was well. She highly doubted the man would accost her on the street when there were so many pedestrians about.

"Yes," she said, discovering her tongue felt thick in her mouth. No man had stirred such a response from her before. It was a novel experience. "I would like that."

Out of courtesy, he offered her his arm, and she placed her hand on his sleeve. The strength she felt beneath her gloved fingers suddenly made her awkward and shy. She paused again after a few steps. "Did I thank you for the flowers?"

"No," he said, sounding unconcerned by her rudeness. "You were too busy trying to reimburse me for the flowers."

Grace winced at her uncharacteristically ungracious behavior. "Then please accept my sincere gratitude. My friend will appreciate them."

The dark-haired gentleman with the easy smile shook his head. "Generous and beautiful," he marveled. "What would you say if I returned to the stall and bought you a bouquet as well?"

Grace clutched Lady Netherley's lilacs to her chest. No gentleman had ever brought her flowers. If she had accepted such a sweet token, she would have plucked a few blooms and pressed them in her favorite book of poetry.

It was with heavy regret in her heart that she shook her head. "I could not impose on you further, sir. Nevertheless, I thank you for the thought."

They had reached the side of her coach. There was no reason for them to continue their light flirtation. The coachman had his hand on the open door and was sizing up her male companion as if he expected trouble from the gentleman.

"Step aside, Yer Lordship," the coachman said, deciding his mistress was too young and foolish not to recognize a fortune hunter when she encountered one. "My lady has appointments to keep."

There was nothing more to say. "Ah, yes . . . I must go. Thank you again for the flowers."

"It is not too late for me to procure a bouquet for you," he said, giving her an excuse to linger if she chose to accept.

"I'll take these, milady," the coachman said, relieving her of the flowers and practically pushing her into the coach. Once he was satisfied that she was settled, he handed her the wrapped bouquet.

"I wish—" She stopped herself before she said something foolish. A lady did not flirt with strangers on the street. Besides, it was unfair to lead this man astray when she needed to settle matters with the Duke of Huntsley. "I really must leave. My friend is expecting me."

The gentleman startled her by grasping her hand. He brought it to his lips and gallantly brushed a kiss against her knuckles. She felt the heat of his lips even through her kid gloves.

"Farewell, my beauty," he said, his voice rough with regret before he released her hand. "Perhaps fate will be merciful and bring us together again."

The coachman deliberately snapped his whip in

the gentleman's direction, forcing the man to leap backward to avoid the stinging lash.

The coach lurched forward, drowning out the gentleman's curses. With her heart weighted with regret, she raised her hand in farewell as she wondered if she would encounter him again.

Grace could not explain the tears that suddenly stung her eyes. She was behaving foolishly. She had just met the gentleman. No one fell in love after a brief flirtation over a bouquet of flowers!

Then why did she want to order the coachman to halt so she could return to the handsome stranger and allow him to purchase her the flowers she so desperately wanted to accept?

The tip of the coachman's whip had struck his hand. *Wily old bastard,* Hunter thought uncharitably as he rubbed the sting from his flesh. So he had bought flowers for a beautiful woman. That was no reason to lash a gent over a harmless flirtation.

Purchasing the flowers had been an impulsive gesture on his part. The blonde had looked troubled as her gaze drifted over the buckets stuffed with flowers; he had wondered if she did not possess the funds to pay for her purchase. He had wanted to do something to make her smile, and she had rewarded him handsomely.

It had been enough.

Or it should have been. In truth, he had been

smitten even before he had glimpsed her face. There was something about the lady that had called to him. Something buried deep in his chest. He absently rubbed the spot over his heart, wishing they had had more time.

It was for the best.

The feeling of loss would pass. If he had desired more from the lady, Hunter would have charmed her into revealing her name so he could see her again. However, his days of flirting with inappropriate females were coming to an end. The sad blonde would have to seek out another gent for comfort. He had a bride to claim.

"The weather is too agreeable to remain indoors, do you not agree?"

Grace turned her head away from the attractive view of Lord and Lady Netherley's town garden to address the elderly marchioness. They were seated at a linen-draped round table one of the servants had procured at her request.

"Indeed, my lady," she said, returning to the table to join her hostess. "Since my arrival, I have been so busy with dress fittings and other tasks that I have missed my daily outdoor walks."

"And I daresay that you need a little more excitement than taking refreshments with an old woman," Lady Netherley said, her knowing expression daring her to protest. "This will simply not do, and you are fortunate to have come to me first. After all, my connections in the *ton* are noteworthy. I would not be exaggerating to say that I know everyone."

"Of this, I have no doubt," murmured Grace, though her response was unnecessary. The elderly marchioness was fully capable of carrying on both sides of the conversation without any assistance from her.

The older woman clasped her hands together with enthusiasm. "Once you have settled into your residence, I would encourage you to tour London's numerous parks and pleasure gardens. If you would prefer, I could arrange an outing with my daughter and daughter-in-law. My girls are slightly older, but I am certain they would be preferable companions rather than spending all of your afternoons with an old fossil like me."

"Nonsense," Grace countered with polite sincerity. "While I will enjoy meeting more of your family, you have the distinct honor of being the first friend that I have made in London. You will soon discover that I do not neglect my friends. Besides, it's rare these days for me to encounter someone who knew my grandfather. Sitting here with you makes me feel closer to him. Does that make any sense, or am I rambling?"

Lady Netherley's eyes glowed with pleasure and approval. "You are a treasure, Lady Grace. Sir Auden would be proud of the lady you have become."

The older woman's praise summoned unexpected tears. Grace weakly smiled at her companion. "Your certainty shames me, Lady Netherley."

"How so, dear?"

Grace picked up her glass of lemonade and took a sip to moisten her dry throat. "Perhaps I should clarify the reasons that have brought me to London." She sipped her lemonade, taking a moment to enjoy the cool tartness. "If you were a friend of my grandfather's, then you are aware of the numerous losses he endured . . . my parents . . . his wife."

Lady Netherley's face softened with sympathy. "I am. If I had not been distracted by my own troubles, I might have been a better friend."

"Over the years, I have read his papers and journals, my lady. Despite the distance, he valued your friendship."

"Thank you, my dear. It is kind of you to ease my guilt. Even so, I blame myself for allowing our friendship to wither when your grandfather was alive. The least I can do is look after his granddaughter."

"Your generosity is overwhelming, Lady Netherley," Grace said, a single tear slipping down her cheek.

The marchioness handed her a handkerchief edged with lace. "There, there. Take this and dry your cheeks. Whatever has brought you to London cannot be insurmountable. I will naturally assist you where I am able, and then there is Hunter."

Grace quieted at the name, clutching the handkerchief in her fist. "Hunter?"

"Why, yes. His Grace, the Duke of Huntsley," the older woman said, sounding mildly surprised. "My friendship with his grandmother goes back to when we were both young ladies, but it's not as if your arranged marriage to Hunter was made in secret. The news even reached London that summer."

So the duke was called Hunter by his friends. It dismayed her to realize how little she knew of the gentleman she was supposed to marry.

Grace lowered her gaze to her lap. "I suspect the Duke of Huntsley will be displeased when he learns that I have traveled to London."

The marchioness made a soft noise of disbelief. "What rubbish! Hunter is a sensible man. There is a wedding to plan, and there is a new wardrobe to consider—" Her eyes widened as a thought occurred to her. The marchioness clapped her hands together in her excitement. "That is it! You and Hunter are planning to wed in town this season. Of course! It is the perfect setting where family and friends can join in the festivities. And the dear boy never said a word . . . the scoundrel!"

Grace studiously admired the lace edges of the handkerchief in her grasp. "The duke is unaware of my arrival, my lady. In fact, he will likely view my presence in town as defiance."

"Defiance?" Lady Netherley said weakly. "Hunter is a reasonable gentleman. Even he would agree that you need a proper wardrobe for London."

Perhaps it had been a mistake to approach the marchioness. Grace sighed. "My wardrobe is the least of his concerns, my lady."

The older woman was disappointed by the news. "Then you have not come to ask my assistance with your wedding."

"Not exactly," Grace said, lifting her gaze and meeting the marchioness's puzzled stare. "I've come to ask your help in ending this betrothal. I wish to sever all ties to the Duke of Huntsley."

Lady Netherley was struck speechless by Grace's declaration. Her mouth parted in amazement and her spine lost some of its aristocratic starch as her back sagged against the back of her chair.

Grace left her seat to kneel in front of the older woman. Gently, she clasped her hand. "Forgive me, I did not mean to upset you. If you wish, I will summon the servant. I did not consider that you might count the duke as one of your friends—"

The marchioness silenced Grace's protests with a dismissive wave of her other hand.

"Oh, do not fret. I am quite well, thank you," Lady Netherley assured her. "So if you manage to free yourself from your arranged marriage, what do you intend to do with your newfound freedom?"

Grace took a sip of her lemonade to wet her dry throat. "This is precisely why I seek your advice, my lady. I have traveled to London in search of a husband."

"Oh good heavens!" Lady Netherley blurted out at Grace's declaration. "Why do you need me to find you a husband when you have a perfectly respectable match arranged?"

"I have it on good authority that His Grace has no interest in honoring the contract," she confessed.

"I do not believe it," the marchioness protested, her voice strengthening with her annoyance. "Despite appearances, Hunter would never dishonor the memory of his grandmother in such a manner. He made a promise to take you as wife, and by all that is holy I will see to it that he does right by you."

"No."

"Good! Then we will—uh, no, you say?" The marchioness called out for her servant. When the man appeared, she said, "Would you be so kind as to bring me my smelling salts?"

Grace glanced warily at her elderly companion. "Lady Netherley?"

The marchioness was in no mood to be coddled. "Do not mind me, child. I have a feeling one of us will need them before our visit has concluded. Now let me see if I understand all of this. You do not wish to marry Hunter."

"What I desire no longer matters," Grace argued. "The Duke of Huntsley has had nineteen years to fulfill the terms of the contract. Do you realize that in all these years, he has never once called on me at Frethwell Hall? Does this sound like the action of an honorable man who intends to do his duty by marrying me? I think not. I could pass him on Bond Street and he would not recognize me."

"But you still wish to marry?"

"Yes. However, it must take place before my twenty-first birthday."

"We have mere weeks to find you a husband," the marchioness mildly protested.

The servant returned with the smelling salts, and she murmured her appreciation as she grasped the small amethyst bottle in her delicate hand.

Sensing she could sway the marchioness, Grace leaned forward. "I am the daughter of a duke and an heiress. Surely, someone with your extraordinary connections could find me a respectable gentleman who is eager to settle down?"

Lady Netherley sighed. "Oh, I could find you a husband, dear girl. That is not the problem."

Puzzled, Grace straightened. "Then what is?"

The marchioness chuckled ruefully. "Is it not obvious? The real challenge will be convincing Hunter to accept your outrageous decision."

Chapter Four

"I can no longer put off the inevitable. I must marry the chit."

The Marquess of Sinclair and the Earl of Rainecourt did not immediately respond to Hunter's announcement. He had been friends with Sin and Reign for so many years, he could barely recall a time when they had not been a part of his life.

Sin stroked his jaw thoughtfully. "And who might this particular chit be? That actress you were dallying with last month? Or are you referring to that rather persistent blonde who appeared smitten with you at Lady Gate's fete? Oh, what was the chit's name? Matilda?" he directed the question to Reign.

"Not a Matilda," Reign countered as he tried to recall the lady's name. "But her name did begin with the letter *M*. Perhaps a Maggie or Minerva?"

Sin grimaced. "Not Minerva. A lady bearing such a name would be too spoiled and long-toothed for our good friend. Sharp elbows."

"What do sharp elbows have to do with anything?"

Hunter demanded, unable to recall ever meeting a brazen blonde at Lady Gate's fete. "And what is this fixation with names that begin with *M*? If this fuzzy-headed logic persists, the two of you might want to abstain from imbibing brandy in the afternoon."

Reign just laughed baldly at what he must have perceived as a jest on Hunter's part. Honestly, was it too much to expect a little support from his friends?

"The lady I was referring is Lady Grace Kearly," he said, unable to conceal the frustration in his voice. "You might recall that I have been pledged to marry the chit, or else I'll lose the inheritance my grandmother bestowed upon me—and may I remind you laughing fools that the house on King Street was one of her properties."

The same house he had donated to the Lords of Vice to create their club Nox. If he failed to marry Lady Grace, his cousin could seize the house and quite possibly assume ownership of the club.

It was a devil of a mess.

And he could use a little support from his friends.

"It's not that we don't appreciate your predicament, gent," Reign said as he tried to catch his breath between laughs. "Nor do we wish to lose Nox over this. I actually had forgotten about the girl. You haven't mentioned her name in years."

His silence was indefensible. Hunter had tried to forget the girl and that he would one day have to marry her or sacrifice his honor and inheritance.

"How do you know she still lives?" Sin inquired.

"After all this time, something could have happened to her. Maybe you have been avoiding a woman who has been dead for years."

"Lady Grace has not succumbed to illness or a convenient accident. Once a year, I send my solicitor to Frethwell Hall on my behalf. He has kept me informed on the lady's welfare."

Hunter could not work up any righteous anger over their amusement or lack of sympathy about his predicament. He rarely uttered Lady Grace's name, even to his closest friends, or mentioned the conditions his grandmother had shackled him with in order to guarantee his compliance.

"Lady Grace turns twenty-one in a few weeks," he calmly explained. At their blank expressions, he added, "According to the arrangement, I must marry the lady before that date elapses, or else I lose part of my inheritance to my cousin Roland Walker."

A man who did not deserve to benefit from Hunter's hard work.

"Ah, Walker, you say," Reign said as recognition lit his dark blue eyes. "I can't recall the last time I encountered the fellow."

"Cutting it a tad close, my friend," Sin observed.

Hunter got up from his chair and paced in front of them while he dragged his hand through his hair. "I am well aware of that fact, Sin. Porter has often scolded me for leaving matters in the air too long. I have attempted to rectify the situation by visiting the lady on several occasions."

"When was this?" Sin asked.

Hunter shook his head. He had not mentioned his failed excursions to anyone. "The dates no longer matter. I was turned away each time because the lady was not in residence."

Reign gave him a level look that had Hunter halting in midstep. "It is unlike you to avoid your responsibilities. You have had years to collect your bride. Why the devil did you tarry? You could have brought her to London last spring. Sophia and Juliana would have been happy to take her in hand, and with Regan, Isabel, and Catherine's assistance, the ladies could have introduced her to London society and given you a chance to become acquainted with the woman you intend to marry."

Juliana and Sophia were Sin's and Reign's wives. Regan was the sister of their mutual friend, the Earl of Chillingsworth. Everyone called him Frost. She was also married to Dare, another member of the Lords of Vice. Isabel was the Earl of Vanewright's wife, and this past summer their friend, the Marquess of Sainthill, had married Lord Greenshield's daughter, Catherine.

Hunter glared at Reign. "I just told you that I tried to see the chit." He had desired a meeting, but he had not considered bringing her to London. Christ, he was such an arse. "You make it sound so simple."

"Do I?" His lips quirked in amusement. "There is nothing simple about courtship."

"I concur," Sin added.

"Courtship?" Hunter tasted the word. "I am marrying the lady. She will be my duchess. I hardly think courting her is necessary."

Both gentlemen shook their heads as if Hunter had disappointed them.

"If you had journeyed to Frethwell Hall years ago as your Porter had advised, you could have saved yourself this misery," Sin said rather unsympathetically.

The two men exchanged glances. Out of the seven Lords of Vice, Sin and Reign had been the first to marry. The rest of them often turned to the gentlemen for guidance when it came to navigating the tricky waters of marriage.

"Last spring was out of the question," Hunter said, knowing he was beginning to sound defensive. "Saint was behaving oddly. He was spending too many nights at the Golden Pearl and—"

"Did you not often join him at the brothel?" Reign interjected.

The question was not meant to be judgmental. Before Reign and the others had found their wives, all of them had enjoyed the company of the exotic and always masked Madame Venna and the pleasures her establishment, the Golden Pearl, had to offer. They had even set up a separate business arrangement at their club, Nox, which was mutually beneficial to both sides.

He should know, since he was the one who sat down with Madame Venna and negotiated the terms with the astute proprietress. It was a pity the woman eventually closed the doors of the elegant brothel. While some of the girls still provided their unique services to Nox, others had disappeared along with their mysterious employer. Madame Venna was sorely missed by her former patrons.

If Saint had his way, her adoring public would never meet her again.

Recalling that Reign was waiting patiently for a reply, Hunter gave up his pacing and claimed one of the chairs. "Naturally. Someone had to watch over him, and you and Sin are no use when it comes to such amusements."

Neither gentleman took offense. Sin picked up the small brass letter opener with a blue enameled handle that someone had left on the table beside him. He tested the point of the ornate blade against the pad of his thumb.

"Those were wild years," Sin admitted, though he discreetly glanced at the door before he spoke. It would have been unfortunate if the ladies had chosen that moment to join them. While Juliana was aware of her husband's former reputation with the ladies, Sin loved his wife beyond distraction and would never have said or done anything that might injure her feelings. "I don't regret them, but I wouldn't trade what I have built with Juliana to revisit them."

"Nor would I," Reign added, his steadfast gaze beginning to make the area between Hunter's shoulder blades itch as his annoyance increased.

Suddenly Hunter could not bear another second of the earl's scrutiny. "Do we have a problem, gents? If you have something to say to me, Reign, I would prefer that you speak plainly."

The only other person who stared at him in that hawkish manner was his grandmother—usually when he had provoked her ire over some trivial mischief or lie.

Sin shrugged when Reign glanced his way. "He's a bit thick-headed, but you can try."

"If this is a private discussion, I'll leave and seek out the ladies. Christ knows they tend to make more sense than you conceited bastards," Hunter said, leaning forward in a feigned attempt to excuse himself.

"Sit down," Reign ordered, and followed it with a firm shove to keep Hunter from standing. "It just isn't my place to interfere, but after watching Saint and Vane muddle through their courtships with their ladies, I feel inclined to spare you the same misery."

"Sensibility. Aye, it's practically the Lords of Vice motto," quipped Sin.

Hunter chuckled. The true motto the Lords of Vice had taken after they had opened Nox was *Virtus Deseritur.* The Latin phrase translated to "virtue is forsaken." It was just one more reason why he had no business marrying an innocent chit like Lady Grace.

If she were still alive, his grandmother would be amused by his predicament.

Reign shot the Sin a warning glance. "Quiet. You

will simply goad him to do the opposite out of sheer stubbornness."

Sin's eyes twinkled as he pointed the letter opener in Hunter's direction. "Now who is doing the goading, eh?"

The earl shook his head in exasperation. "Ignore him," he told Hunter. "I just wanted to offer you some advice. Be kind to her."

Hunter scowled at his friend. There was no doubt Reign was speaking of Lady Grace. "That's your grand advice? Be kind? Of course I'll be kind to her. What sort of man do you think I am?"

"A great man," Reign replied instantly, which slightly mollified Hunter. "You have kindness in you, not to mention humor, intelligence, and an appreciation of savoring life to the fullest."

Sensing the earl was faltering in his explanation, Sin interjected, "What Reign is trying to say is that he—both of us, actually—are concerned about you and the girl if you plan to honor this arranged marriage your grandmother brokered with her family. It is a difficult situation, to be certain, and it would be unfair to blame the poor girl for something her grandfather instigated."

Hunter gaped at his friends. "Both of you are half-wits. I've never struck a woman in my life!" he thundered, insulted by the suggestion that he would physically harm the lady.

"Hunter . . ." Sin said, sighing. "You've banished the girl for most of her life to the country. I cannot presume to speak for the lady; if given the choice, however, you have little interest in seeing your grandmother's grand plans through. Perhaps you should consider forfeiting your inheritance so you and Lady Grace—"

"No," he said unequivocally.

"What kind of marriage will the two of you have?" Reign pressed. His calm logic did little to soothe Hunter's temper. "Admit it. You haven't even met Lady Grace, and yet you despise her."

Hunter lowered his heated gaze. "That's a strong response to a lady I have not seen since we were children." Belatedly, he thought to add, "And for the record, I don't despise her."

Not exactly.

His friends also knew that he wasn't telling the truth.

It was not his fault that for many years just the thought of losing his freedom to a woman who was not of his choosing, caused bile to rise in his throat.

"Truly?" Sin smirked. "You have spent most of your life bedding every female who tossed herself at you. Not precisely the actions of a gentleman betrothed to a duke's daughter."

"You're quite the dissembler," he replied, resisting the urge to tackle Sin and pummel him into the rug. "After all, you are accusing me of misdeeds that you are equally guilty of. More so, since you shagged more females than all of us combined. How many ladies did you bestow pearl necklaces upon to win

their favors? Wouldn't your wife be furious if she
heard the answer from your lips?"

Sin's eyes flared with fury. Hunter silently marveled at his friend's restraint. If he had spoken this
way to Saint, there was a good chance Hunter would
have been flat on his back while he checked for loose
teeth.

Instead, Sin yelled, "I, on the other hand, was *not*
betrothed to anyone, so what I did, how often, and
with how many women does not apply. Christ, you
are a righteous bastard!"

Reign held up both hands to keep the two men in
their seats. "Gents, please . . . the past no longer matters." Satisfied that Sin was not planning to throttle
anyone, the earl turned to Hunter. "Although I rarely
speak of it, of all the Lords of Vice, you are aware
that I am the only one intimately acquainted with
how empty a loveless marriage is. It eats at a man's
soul, and no amount of brandy, mistresses, or reck-
lessness will offer peace. So when I ask you to reconsider your decision, it is because I think of you as
my brother and do not wish to watch you suffer as I
once did."

Hunter remained silent. Reign rarely spoke of
his first marriage to Beatrice Roberts. It had ended
badly for the couple. There had been rumors that her
parents had urged her to accept the young earl's betrothal, even while her heart belonged to another.
One terrible night, after an evening of drinking and
fighting, the seven-months-pregnant countess was

found dead in her bedchamber. For many years, Reign feared he was responsible for her death. He had been so drunk, he could not recall what had transpired that evening.

To this day, there were a few in the *ton* who still wondered if he had had a hand in murdering her.

"I won't do anything reckless," Hunter said quietly. "It is why I thought it best that I journey to Frethwell Hall instead of inviting Lady Grace to London. Porter tells me that the lady has an agreeable disposition. Even so, I have been warned by the man on several occasions that I can take nothing for granted. It has been conveyed that she is somewhat displeased by what is perceived as my neglect. If Lady Grace will not have me, then perhaps your and Sin's concern is for naught."

Reign offered him a half smile. "Perhaps."

Hunter offered his hand in apology to Sin. Thankfully, the marquess accepted it without hesitation. "Do you have some advice on how I might get back in the lady's good graces?"

"I might," Sin said, releasing Hunter's hand. "Though do not count on the task to be simple. A mistress can be swayed by flattery and expensive baubles. A lady worthy of marriage will demand a higher price to restore her honor."

Hunter made a soft scoffing noise. "What lady concerns herself with honor?"

"One worth fighting to keep," Reign replied.

* * *

Rosemary greeted Grace upon her return.

"How was your meeting with Lady Netherley? Did it go well?"

Grace untied the bow under her chin and carefully removed her bonnet. She handed her it to her companion. "Our visit was amiable, though I did manage to startle her when she learned the reasons for my journey to London."

Rosemary made a soft clicking sound with her tongue as she gathered up the dangling ribbons and tucked them into the bonnet. "I'll wager she was. And what was Her Ladyship's response?"

Grace handed over her gloves. "I have her support. However, she warned me that Hunter might be a concern."

"Hunter," Rosemary said, her eyebrows lifting in curiosity at her lady's affectionate abbreviation of the duke's name.

"It is what his family and friends call the duke," Grace defensively replied, ignoring the abrupt pang in her heart. She had been betrothed to him for most of her young life and she had not known he was called Hunter. "Lady Netherley sympathized with my reasons when I explained the why of it. Nevertheless, she went on to explain that the duke was quite close to his grandmother and this marriage arrangement was important to her."

"And your grandfather, sweet."

Grace nodded reluctantly. "Yes. It was important to my grandfather as well." Her encounters with her uncle had proven that the gentleman could not be trusted.

Together she and Rosemary ascended the narrow staircase. "Lady Netherley recommended that I approach the Duke of Huntsley before I hire a solicitor."

Her friend sighed with disappointment. "So the marchioness will not help you."

"On the contrary, I have the lady's support either way." Grace raised her skirt higher as she climbed the last step. "As the daughter of a duke, Lady Netherley assures me that I shall fare very well with the *ton*. Once I have secured the duke's consent to dissolve the marriage contract, she is quite confident that she can find me a husband before my twenty-first birthday."

"Truly?" Rosemary asked, sounding surprised. "And are you so eager to marry?"

Grace smiled in an attempt to ease her friend's concern. "Not particularly," she said carelessly. "I have spent most of my life preparing to be a proper duchess for the Duke of Huntsley. I have not given much thought to a life without the burden of the title or the man who cannot bear my very presence. On the other hand, I have no desire to trade one master for another. With the duke out of the way, my uncle will seize my lands and fortune, while he prays for a timely accident to claim my life."

"Temper your tongue while you reside in London," Rosemary whispered. "You are accusing a duke of plotting your murder."

Grace shrugged. "He has been accused of worse,"

she said, recalling some of her grandfather's conversations over the years. "Though it might not come to that. All my uncle would have to do is lock me away in the country or marry me off to a gentleman of *his* choosing."

She would prefer to live her life as a spinster than submit to a gentleman who was under her uncle's thumb. "Once I free myself of the Duke of Huntsley, I will be at liberty to marry a gentleman of my choosing. Rosemary, I will finally be free."

"Not quite," Rosemary said, dousing Grace's enthusiasm as effectively as pouring water on the kitchen coals. "You are too young to appreciate this bit of wisdom, but I love you too much not to say it. There is no such thing as freedom, my girl. Not the sort you are dreaming about. We are all tethered in numerous ways: family, duty, expectations of our neighbors, need to fill your empty belly—"

The older woman held up her hand to silence the protest rising in Grace. "Now, I am not trying to convince you one way or the other. If you want to walk away from this marriage arrangement between you and the duke, you have my full support. And you have a friend in Lady Netherley, which is helpful since all of London is filled with the Duke of Huntsley's friends."

She made it sound as if Grace were treading onto enemy territory. "Rosemary . . . His Grace has done his duty by looking after my inheritance, but he has ignored *me* for nineteen years. He will most likely be relieved that I am willing to cry off."

"One would think, but I know men. They can be territorial about their possessions."

"Don't be absurd!" Grace moved her shoulder to shrug off Rosemary's hand. She continued down the hall. "I am no man's possession."

Certainly not the Duke of Huntsley's!

The very thought made the fine hair on her arms prickle. "You will see that I am right when I work up the courage to confront him."

Perhaps she should seek out Mr. Porter first. With him and Lady Netherley at her side, the Duke of Huntsley would temper his responses to her generous offer.

"Just remember, most men do not respond well to the unexpected. And you, my sweet girl, are definitely unlike any lady His Grace has encountered."

Grace halted, wondering if her friend meant that as a compliment. "I do not care if I give *Hunter* indigestion. I just want to be released from my obligation to him."

Chapter Five

Her first London ball.

Grace could barely contain her excitement as she stood next to Lady Netherley and her youngest daughter, Lady Ellen Courtland. The two ladies had invited her to join them in their coach this evening so she would not have to enter Lord and Lady Lovelace's town house without an escort.

She wished Rosemary could have shared this adventure with her. While her former nursemaid was an agreeable companion at Frethwell Hall, she would never be accepted by the *ton*. Her and Rosemary's differences were more apparent in London, and though Grace understood, she wished she had been in a position to change the rules.

"Are you nervous?" Lady Ellen whispered in Grace's ear after they had paid their respects to the earl and his countess. At nine-and-twenty, the youngest child of Lord and Lady Netherley was as independent and incorrigible as her mother. She was an unrepentant spinster, much to the dismay of her family.

Nonetheless, Grace had already deduced that the lady's unmarried state was not due to the lack of suitors. Lady Ellen had numerous admirers. It was a subject she hoped to one day discuss in great detail with her.

"Am I nervous? Not at all," Grace replied as she surveyed the ballroom.

"There is no shame in being anxious," her new friend continued. "After all, if Mama has her way, she will have half a dozen gentlemen vying for your hand by evening's end."

Grace was heartened by the news.

"Hush, Ellen," Lady Netherley lightly scolded her daughter. "If I proved to be so successful, I would have had you married off years ago."

Lady Ellen rolled her eyes, having heard this old lament on countless occasions. "If you are as clever as you appear to be, Lady Grace, you should run before my mother tosses you to the lions."

"Honestly, daughter." The elderly marchioness placed her hand on Lady Ellen's arm as they promenaded the circumference of the ballroom. "Where do you come up with such notions? If you had any sense, you would tell the dear girl that you are merely jesting."

Grace idly wondered if Lady Netherley was holding on to her daughter for much-needed support or if it was to prevent the young woman from dashing off.

Lady Ellen grinned down at her mother. "But that would be a lie, would it not, Mama?"

Lady Netherley shook her head in feigned disappointment. "You're an insolent child."

Grace walked beside them when it was possible, and when it was not she trailed after them. Earlier, when the marchioness was not berating her daughter over her unfortunate unmarried state, she had announced that her son and daughter-in-law would be meeting them at the ball.

"I do my best," Lady Ellen said cheerfully. She turned her face toward Grace and whispered, "I wasn't jesting. Consider yourself duly warned."

It was an odd statement, coming from a lady she barely knew. Then again, it was apparent within minutes of sitting in the coach with the two women that Lady Ellen found her mother's attempts at matchmaking tiresome. Perhaps she thought Grace would react in the same manner.

"I am looking forward to meeting all of your family and friends," Grace said sincerely.

Lady Ellen chuckled. "Such an innocent. Let's see if you feel the same way on the drive home, eh?"

"Ellen, I believe Lady Child is attempting to get your attention," Lady Netherley said, sensing it was time to change the subject.

The young woman glanced in the direction her

mother was gesturing toward. "No she is n—" Lady Ellen bit her lower lip and raised her hand in greeting. "If I hadn't been standing beside you, I could swear you did this deliberately."

Bewildered by the resignation in her companion's voice, Grace asked, "Is something amiss?"

Lady Ellen pouted. "Lady Child has a younger son and a nephew she would like to get rid of."

"Ears, my dear daughter . . . ears," Lady Netherley muttered.

"Her Ladyship does not care which one I marry. And if it was legal, she would probably insist that I marry both of them," she confided, but softened her voice to appease her mother.

"Oh." Grace tipped her head to the side and noticed that Lady Child was still beckoning Lady Ellen to join her and a very sallow-colored gentleman. "You have my sympathies."

"Indeed." Lady Ellen lifted her chin and squared her shoulders. "Perhaps I could convince Vane to challenge the whole family. Such an insult should free me from the lady's tender hooks."

"I forbid you to speak to Vane or Isabel about Lady Child or her family," the marchioness said, stabbing her walking stick into the wooden floor to stress her dictate.

"Don't fret, Mama." Lady Ellen kissed her mother's cheek. "For your sake, I won't speak to Vane about it this evening. I will meet up with you later." To Grace, she said, "Best of luck with the lions!"

Grace contemplated the woman's parting words as she observed her greeting Lady Child and her son in a friendly manner. Or was the gentleman the lady's nephew?

"What did she mean about the lions?" She looked at the marchioness when she did not respond right away.

"Nothing. My youngest has an odd sense of humor," Lady Netherley said, taking her by the arm and leading her in the opposite direction. "In truth, my son suffers from the same affliction so you have my permission to ignore him, too. Heaven knows if I had listened to half the things he said, I would have never bothered introducing him to his wife."

"I see." Grace was uncertain how to respond. It appeared the entire family comprised odd fellows. Perhaps her faith in Lady Netherley had been misplaced?

"Come along, my dear," the marchioness said, her wizened face brightening as she recognized several people in the distance. "This has all the promise of an intriguing evening!"

Hunter had less charitable thoughts about his evening.

Earlier in the afternoon, he had received troubling news from the messenger he had sent to Frethwell Hall. His intention had been to alert the household of his upcoming visit so preparations could be made in advance. Instead, he learned that Lady Grace was not in residence. According to the butler, his mistress had taken residence in London since she was in the market for a husband.

A husband. Had the silly chit forgotten that she was betrothed to *him*?

He could not decide which upset him more—the notion that Lady Grace was ignoring rules he had established for her protection, or her determination to find another gentleman to take his place.

Lady Grace had placed herself in peril by traveling to London on her own. Not only were there brigands and scoundrels to contend with, but she did not have a single friend in town who might offer her shelter. A wealthy lady drew all sorts of unsavory attention, and for that alone he could quietly strangle her with his bare hands.

The chit was a lamb in a town of wolves.

Working feverishly to pick up her trail, it had taken Hunter's men three hours to deduce that Lady Grace was not without resources or friends. He should have guessed that Lady Netherley would embrace the lost little lamb.

The marchioness was also the one lady who had a certain reputation as a matchmaker. Had Lady Grace asked the elderly woman for assistance in securing a husband this season?

And what would have been Lady Netherley's response to such a request? Vane's mother was too kindhearted to turn away a lady in need. Of course she would help her. There was no doubt that Lady

Grace viewed him with a jaundiced eye, and the marchioness had likely heard rumors of Hunter's conquests while she resided in town.

Saint and Catherine had been visiting when Hunter had received the news of his errant bride-to-be. His first inclination was to confront Lady Netherley immediately, and scold her for her part in this mischief. Saint advised against this. The marchioness was Vane's mother, and he did not take kindly to anyone upsetting her. Catherine also recommended caution when handling his reluctant betrothed. If Lady Grace was preparing to contest the arranged marriage, she might flee, and this time she might not find herself among friends. Saint concurred.

Outnumbered, Hunter had not rushed over to the Netherleys' town house to demand Lady Grace's whereabouts. Saint vowed that he and Catherine would call on the marchioness on his behalf.

A messenger arrived at the door an hour later with a note from his friend. Lady Netherley had not been at home, but Saint assured him that he would send word after he spoke to the lady.

Hunter was still waiting.

He had discovered during the past few hours that he was slightly offended that Lady Netherley had not sought him out immediately when Lady Grace had presented herself at her door. It was simple enough to conclude that the marchioness had a few things to say about his dastardly neglect of the lady.

At this moment, was Lady Netherley introducing

Hunter's betrothed to potential suitors in the hope of finding her a proper husband?

The casual thought made him itch to punch something.

Hunter supposed he would be forced to endure a stern lecture from Lady Netherley before she allowed him to see Lady Grace. She would have reminded him that this mess was of his own making. If he had courted Lady Grace as she had deserved, the lady would have been a part of their lives long ago. They most likely would have already married, and his promise to his grandmother would have been kept.

And the best part of all would have been his cousin's disappointment. His chance to steal Hunter's inheritance would have expired once he had married and bedded his duchess.

If it had been anyone else besides Vane's sweet, generous mother, he would have demanded Lady Grace's whereabouts and secured his betrothed within the hour. Once he applied for a special license, he would put an end to her nonsense of marrying another gent.

Instead of collecting his bride, Hunter was sitting in Lord Clement's study with Reign, Dare, and Sin only halfheartedly paying attention to the cards in front of him. His thoughts had drifted to several streets over, where according to Sin, Lady Netherley was likely to make an appearance since she was a good friend of Lady Lovelace.

"Don't think about it," Sin advised, not glancing up from the cards in his hand.

"I have no idea what you are talking about," Hunter replied, feigning innocence.

Dare seemed to have the advantage this evening since he was winning. His turn did not distract him from the conversation. "I believe Sin is referring to your desire to ignore everyone's advice and attend Lord and Lady Lovelace's ball."

He scowled at the worthless hand he had been dealt. Blast it, at this rate Dare was going to beggar them all.

"I would not recommend it," Reign said, giving him a knowing glance. "Charging into the ballroom and berating Vane's mother for some imagined slight will serve no purpose."

"It will make me feel better," Hunter said defiantly. "And the slight isn't imagined. Lady Netherley should have had the decency to let me know my bride was in town."

"Clearly the lady had her own reasons not to tell you," Dare mused. "Humiliating her in front of the *ton* will not coax her to support your side."

"Not to mention, Vane will cut out your tongue for upsetting his mother," Sin pointed out.

"I haven't upset anyone. Yet." Disgusted with his cards and the conversation, Hunter folded and slapped his cards facedown on the table. "No coaxing will be required when I get my hands on Lady Grace. She will obey me."

Sin, Dare, and Reign chuckled.

Dare shook his head at Hunter's lack of understanding. "My friend, I would refrain from using such words as *obey* until you have married the girl."

Reign nodded. "Women are contrary creatures. They tend to do the opposite when provoked."

Hunter raised his hands in mock surrender. "I am a reasonable gentleman. As long as the chit behaves, we will get along."

Sin pointed a finger at him. "You have never been reasonable when it comes to this young lady. You can barely stomach speaking her name out loud."

"Don't be ridiculous," Hunter scoffed, ignoring the fact that what the marquess said was essentially the truth. "Lady Grace. There. See. Are you satisfied?"

"Aye. But you'll never be if you keep behaving like an arse," Sin said, and all three men had a good laugh over what they perceived as Hunter's lack of understanding of women.

Well, he had had enough.

Hunter stood up. "I'm heading over there. There's no harm in paying my respects to the Lovelaces. Lady Netherley won't even know I'm there."

Well, unless Lady Grace was also in attendance. If the lady was at the marchioness's side, then no one could stop him from approaching her.

Sin abandoned his cards. "I'm joining you."

"Me, too," said Reign, willing to accept his losses.

"Fine lot of friends, you are. I'm winning," Dare complained.

Hunter glared at his friend. "Are you coming or not?"

"Aye, I'm coming," grumbled Dare. "My wife is attending the ball so I might as well join her. What's more, I doubt you will be able to just observe your lady. You're going to need us to distract Lady Netherley if you are planning to steal her from under her chaperone's nose."

Chapter Six

There were so many names to remember.

No one would have ever accused Grace of being shy, but after of hours of introductions, even she was feeling overwhelmed.

"Considering how many gentlemen have begged me for an introduction, you'll need to order several new pairs of evening slippers," Lady Netherley said after one of the gentlemen escorted her back to her circle of new friends. She could not recall his name, but he had only stepped on her toes once during the energetic country dance.

"It will be worth it," Grace said, silently wishing they could find a place to sit.

"Slightly overwhelming, is it not?" said the petite brunette who was poised to her right. "Don't fret. In a month, you will have committed everyone's names to heart."

The tall blonde beside her with the blue-green eyes laughed. "And likely know all their secrets."

Grace nodded, struggling to match names within

their small group. The brunette was Lady Pashley. The elderly marchioness explained that the lady was married to one of the duke's friends. The blonde with the elegant walking stick was also connected to the Lords of Vice. Lady Netherley explained that the woman had suffered a grievous injury as a child, which damaged her eyesight. Though her gaze did seem a little unfocused on occasion, Grace would have never guessed the young countess was struggling with partial blindness.

"I feel foolish," she confided to the blonde. "What was your name again?"

Understanding and something akin to sympathy flickered in her gaze. "It is unnecessary to apologize. I am Lady Rainecourt, though you may call me Sophia since we will soon be family."

Lady Pashley brought her hand to her heart. "And I am Regan."

Grace blushed at the word *family*. Although both ladies had deliberately refrained from mentioning the Duke of Huntsley's name, marriage to him was the only way she could be connected to these women.

"How are you related to the duke?" she asked.

"Am I related to Hunter?" Regan wrinkled her nose in amusement. "No. My brother is the Earl of Chillingsworth. When Lady Netherley speaks of Frost, she is referring to my brother."

"Juliana and Isabel, whom you met earlier, Regan, and myself are married to gentlemen who have been friends most of their lives. The *ton* calls them the Lords of Vice—"

"I beg your pardon," Grace interrupted, wondering if she had misunderstood her companion. "You and Sophia are married to gentlemen who call themselves the Lords of Vice?"

Sophia responded before Regan could explain. "Several very vexed members of the *ton* began to call them that awful name when they were more boys than men."

"Hunter is one of the seven," Regan said as she held up her hand to count off the names of the remaining men. "Then there is my husband, Dare; my brother; Sophia's Reign; Juliana's husband, Sin; Lady Netherley's son, Vane; and Saint. He's married to Catherine, though I doubt the couple will be attending the Lovelaces' ball this evening."

"Astounding," Grace marveled. She had learned more about the Duke of Huntsley and his friends in one evening than she had gleaned from Mr. Porter during the last nineteen years. "And your husbands and the others do not mind being called the Lords of Vice?"

"When you get to know them, you will see the sobriquet is wholly appropriate," Regan added.

Sophia tilted her head to concur. "True. Over the years, the men have become more than friends, and now that many of them have gone on to marry and beget children, we have all become family."

"You will feel the same, once you marry Hunter," Regan said blithely.

Grace bit her lower lip. She had asked Lady Netherley not to share her plans before she had confronted the duke. If Hunter had refrained from sharing his personal business with his friends, then the ladies were unaware that the duke was not interested in her or marriage.

"Am I interrupting something?"

Grace glanced at the handsome dark-haired gentleman who approached them with an air of familiarity. One of the ladies' husbands, perhaps?

"If I said *yes,* would you leave us?" Regan teased.

The gentleman tapped her lightly on her nose. "On the contrary, I would have regretted not joining you sooner."

"I am amazed you stayed away this long," Sophia said with a hint of a smile playing across her mouth.

No, he was not married to either woman. There was a casual intimacy among them, but he behaved as if he were talking to annoying female relatives. Was this Regan's brother? The one she called Frost?

If so, it also meant that he was another one of the duke's good friends. And she had hoped to gain the advantage over Hunter by learning more about him, but how could she best him when she was outnumbered and surrounded by his closest friends?

Her predicament did not bode well for her.

The gentleman continued, unaware of her increasing discomfort. "When I arrived, Juliana was the first to warn me off. Lady Netherley was the second. It was then that I knew I just had to meet your beautiful companion."

Suddenly Grace had become the center of attention.

The gentleman stared at her boldly, almost as thoroughly as if he had touched her. She felt the impact of his unique turquoise-blue gaze like a warm wave sweeping from her face and spreading out over her chest. The corners of his mouth quirked as if he had guessed her reaction to his interest.

"Perhaps you should have listened to Juliana and the marchioness," Regan said, sounding exasperated.

"When have I ever listened to anyone?" the gentleman countered. "Will you perform the introduction or shall I deepen that pretty blush on the lady's cheeks by impressing her with my daring?"

Regan rolled her eyes as she lightly touched Grace on the arm. "Forgive my brother, Lady Grace. We have tried to civilize him, but his head is as dense as granite."

"As is my heart, though I endeavor to find a lady who might persuade me to make an exception," he said, the blue in his gaze darkening as he admired her from head to toe. "You may call me Frost."

"Oh, dear," Sophia softly muttered to no one in particular.

Regan noticed Grace's wary expression, and added to ease her concern about her brazen sibling, "Lady Grace Kearly, may I present my older brother, the

Earl of Chillingsworth. Forgive his boldness. He believes he is being charming."

"I *am* charming," Frost said smoothly. "Do you not agree, Lady Grace?"

It was probably a bad notion to encourage the earl, but she could not prevent herself from smiling at his arrogance. She inclined her head as she curtsied. "Has anyone dared to disagree with you, Lord Chillingsworth?"

Frost drew attention with his sudden bark of laughter. "Very few are that courageous, my lady. But I occasionally enjoy the novelty of it." He bowed gallantly. "So whom do you belong to, Lady Grace?"

Regan and Sophia seemed displeased by the question.

Grace was also distrustful of the gentleman's intentions. "I belong to myself, Lord Chillingsworth." Since that sounded odd, even to her ears, she explained, "I was orphaned when I was very young."

Grace required no sympathy from anyone. She had been so young when her mother and father had died that she did not remember them. All she had to cling to were the stories her grandfather and Rosemary told her, and old paintings in the gallery at Frethwell Hall.

The earl nodded, deducing that any sympathy would not have been welcome. "Ah, yes . . . and if I recall correctly, you are the Duke of Strangham's daughter."

Surprise lit up her eyes. "My uncle inherited the

title, but your assumptions are correct. How did you know? You must have been a child when my father and mother died."

Then it occurred to her. The Duke of Huntsley had shared certain details of her life with his friends.

Instead of mentioning his connection to Hunter, he explained, "Oh, I was a boy. However, you come from an old and revered family, Lady Grace. The loss of your parents touched many hearts in the *ton,* and such losses are often discussed and lamented by our elders."

It was a reasonable explanation, and it touched her heart that the *ton* had not forgotten her parents as she had. Unfortunately for the earl, she did not believe that was the true source of his knowledge about her personal tragedy.

"I did not expect to encounter you so late at the Lovelaces'," Regan said, her eyes narrowing with suspicion. "You usually get bored at these affairs."

"I do," her brother said in agreeable tones. To Grace, he confessed, "Greedy hostesses are reluctant to allow wealthy bachelors to slip through their fingers."

Regan appeared to surrender. "Not exactly subtle, dear brother. I can think of a certain gentleman who will not appreciate your mischief."

Was his sister referring to Hunter? Grace's lips parted as she prepared to assure her companions that the Duke of Huntsley had not concerned himself with the personal details of her life.

However, she held her tongue as Sophia's laughter drew everyone's attention to her. "If you wish to leave, I suspect Lady Lovelace would make an exception for you, Frost," she teased.

"You are probably right, lovely Sophia," the earl said, attempting to appear contrite. "Which, of course, is just one more reason to remain. Do you not agree, Lady Grace?"

It was difficult not to like Lord Chillingsworth. Especially when he was trying so hard to win her favor.

"Would you consider it daring of me to disagree, my lord?" she asked flirtatiously.

"Indeed," he said, moving closer. "My favorite kind of lady."

"Frost," Regan said, a crisp reprimand infused in the single word.

The earl's scrutiny of her face did not falter. "Do not ask me to behave, dear sister. It's simply not in my nature."

"Lord Chillingsworth, what are you doing?" Lady Netherley demanded as she quickened her stride to break up any mischief.

"Why, nothing at all, dear lady—yet," he drawled.

The elderly marchioness's response was one of predictable indignation on the behalf of the young lady for whom she felt a certain responsibility.

"Well, you wicked man, you will cease this instant!" Lady Netherley raised her walking stick to bar the earl from stepping closer. "Lady Grace is under my protection. I suggestion you tarry with the ladies who are not!"

Lord Chillingsworth brought his fist to his heart. "My dear Lady Netherley, you wound me with your assumptions."

It was apparent there was affection between the earl and the marchioness.

"I know what you are about," the older woman said fiercely. "And I will not tolerate it."

The earl astounded everyone by extending his hand to Grace. "My lady, will you honor me with a dance?"

Sophia frowned and Regan sighed. Apparently, no one expected Lord Chillingsworth to extend the invitation.

Lady Netherley did not mince her words. "Do you think the gossips will hold their tongues?"

The poor woman was worried about the Duke of Huntsley's reaction to the news. It was on the tip of Grace's tongue to tell the marchioness that her concerns were for naught. The duke did not care what she did as long as she remained in her gilt cage.

If she had been aware that it was rare for the earl to invite any lady to dance, Grace might have questioned the wisdom in accepting his offer. Blissfully unaware, she slipped her hand into Lord Chillingsworth's. "I would be honored, my lord."

The course already set, none of women said another word of protest as Grace strolled away with the gentleman most of the *ton* thought was the wickedest of all the Lords of Vice.

Chapter Seven

Hunter entered the Lord and Lady Lovelace's ball-room intent on finding his quarry.

Lady Netherley.

He was prepared to behave as long as the marchioness revealed Lady Grace's whereabouts. If she refused, then the evening might take an unpleasant turn.

Recognizing that particular expression on his friend's face, Sin attempted to thwart what was likely to develop into a confrontation. "It might be prudent to find our ladies, first. I'll wager Juliana, as well as the others, have sought an introduction to Lady Grace if she is present this evening. Perhaps they will be able to direct you to her so you do not have to intimidate Vane's mother or fondle every unfamiliar lady in the ballroom."

"With most of the Lords of Vice in attendance, I can predict how this evening will end—with us getting tossed out of the Lovelaces' ball. It will be the highlight of our evening," quipped Dare. "Regan will blister our ears for ruining what she considers her efforts to improve on our reputation."

Hunter laughed, viewing the lady's efforts as a hopeless task. The people surrounding them respected wealth and power. He would leave the etiquette and charity to the ladies.

"It isn't a jest," Reign said, shouldering his way among them. "Our wives have to hold their heads up in this town. Being married to the Lords of Vice cannot make it an easy task."

Hunter disagreed, and was prepared to debate the issue with Reign. However, the man kept walking, uninterested in anyone else's opinion on the subject. Sin shrugged and followed.

"Only a weak-minded fool would allow a woman to dictate his life," he complained to Dare.

Dare grinned at him. "Spoken like a gent with nothing to lose or a sleepy, well-pleasured lady in his bed each night."

Now his friend was being cruel. "Who says I want a female in my bed each night?"

The marquess gave him a look of disbelief. "If you don't give a farthing one way or the other, why precisely are you in a lather about Lady Grace?"

Hunter's jaw tightened, but he kept his mouth shut.

Dare gave him a knowing grin. "That's what I thought you'd say, my friend. Come on, let's find Lady Netherley before you offend the wrong person."

* * *

"You enjoyed the dance."

Grace heard the indulgent satisfaction in Lord Chillingsworth's voice, but she could not deduce a reason for it.

"How could I not with you as my partner?" she said as they walked together. She had thought the earl would return her promptly to Lady Netherley to prove that he could be trusted.

However, her companion was not ruled by anyone. She rather liked that about him.

"Do you want to step outside?" he asked, already nudging her toward the open doors.

"I would not mind some fresh air. It's a little stuffy in here," she said, smiling up at him. "Can I ask you something, Lord Chillingsworth?"

"Anything . . . if you call me Frost."

The scoundrel. He thought nothing of flirting with a lady who was betrothed to one of his closest friends. The man was shameless.

"Well, Frost, would you consider yourself an honest gentleman?"

Amusement flickered in his gaze. "Sometimes. When it serves me to be so. Why do you ask?"

"For the usual reasons," she said brightly. "I have a question and wondered if you would give me an honest answer."

The earl halted abruptly, and belatedly Grace realized that they were alone. "A challenge. Go ahead, Lady Grace. Ask your question."

Perhaps she should have asked Regan or Sophia.

Still, she was no coward. "I have met several of your friends and their wives this evening. All of you have one person in common, and yet all of you have studiously avoided speaking his name. Why is that?"

His white teeth flashed as he smiled at her. "You are wondering why no one has mentioned the Duke of Huntsley, eh? I cannot speak for the others, though I am not surprised by their reluctance."

"How so?"

Frost held her in place when she tried to continue their stroll. "You are incredibly beautiful. If Hunter had known, he might have reconsidered abandoning you to the country."

"Is that what he told you?"

"My darling lady, Hunter never mentions you at all." He noted her pained expression and sighed. "And that is why my good friends have avoided uttering the gent's name. Everyone is uncertain of your plans, and no one wishes to injure your feelings."

"You know, don't you?"

"That you seek to dissolve this arranged marriage? Yes?"

"Lady Netherley promised not to speak of it," she said, furious at herself for confiding in the marchioness. It had been a calculated risk, but she had thought the elderly woman's friendship with Grace's grandfather would encourage her to honor her word.

"Don't you be angry at the marchioness," he said in the ensuing silence. "She has known Hunter since he was a lad, and feels you would be better off under his care."

She did not bother concealing her skepticism. "And do you agree?"

"Let's just say that I have an aversion to the notion of marriage. Hunter has protected you for nineteen years; if he chooses he could continue to do so without the messy complication of a loveless union," the earl said pragmatically.

Grace was conflicted. Lord Chillingsworth was the first person in London who genuinely supported her position, and yet she felt strangely insulted that he did not approve of the match with his friend.

"Do you think His Grace has formed a similar opinion?" she asked.

"You will have to ask him yourself," he said dismissively as if he did not care either way. He stepped closer, his body blocking the filtered light from the ballroom. "However, I will share my thoughts if you are interested?"

"Of course."

"Do not marry Hunter," he said bluntly. "My friend is capable of appreciating your beauty and body, but you will never claim his love. You are so young . . . innocent. It is the folly of youth to reach for the unattainable, and you will spend the rest of your life regretting it."

She could barely swallow as she contemplated the lonely years of being bound to a man who could never love her. "I—thank you for your honesty, Frost. Unfortunately, I happen to agree with you."

"I have another confession to make," Lord Chillingsworth said, his fingers lightly stroking the flesh just above her elbows. "Truth is as deadly as a double-edged sword, and you inspire me to play fairly with you."

Grace stilled, sensing his words were important. "You do not always play fairly, my lord?"

"I avoid it at all costs," he admitted. "Do you want to know why I approached you this evening, when I had been warned off by several of my friends?"

"Why?"

His chin tipped upward as he found his thoughts amusing. "I generally abhor innocent misses like you. No offense, my dear, but you and your dewy-eyed peers are nothing but trouble. And there lies my quandary. My nature is to indulge all of my senses in the forbidden, and you, Lady Grace, most definitely are as tempting as the red, shiny apple was to Adam in the Garden of Eden. I shouldn't—" He gave her an apologetic look.

Puzzled, she asked, "Should not do what?"

"This."

The teasing caress of his fingers unexpectedly transformed into iron manacles on her upper arms. He pulled her up against his body, and covered her protest with a kiss. Though he made no attempt to deepen the kiss, his mouth was warm and firm against hers.

He released her just as quickly.

Grace stumbled backward and gaped at the earl. "Is this the part where I'm supposed to slap you in the face and then march back into the ballroom alone?" She wondered if this had been his plan all along, though she could not fathom his motives.

Was he trying to ruin her reputation?

"I have another suggestion," he said, his turquoise-blue gaze gleaming. "Come closer and kiss me again."

"No," Grace said, appalled by his suggestion. Lord Chillingsworth was clearly not to be trusted. "Why did you kiss me?"

"Answer a question first."

"I think I've answered enough of your questions."

He ignored her evasion, and asked, "Am I the first man to kiss you?"

Grace laughed nervously. "I have no intention of giving you a reply to such a rude question."

The earl inclined his head, and for a moment she thought he would attempt to kiss her again, but he diverted course and leaned close enough for his lips to brush her ear.

"You already have, my darling girl," he whispered, sending shivers down her arms and back. "No, don't ruin it by feigning outrage. We both know you enjoyed it. Permit me the small victory that I was the first gent to kiss you."

Grace took a deep breath as she prepared to tell Lord Chillingsworth what an arrogant blackguard he was—but then she changed her mind. While he deserved a slap and a good scolding, she refused to deliver the rebuke he expected from her.

Instead she brazenly turned her face toward his. Their lips were mere inches apart. "Why should I complain?" she replied. "You are old and experienced enough to be aware that your kisses are quite extraordinary."

"Shall we stroll deeper into the Lovelaces' back gardens?"

"A bit too daring for me, I confess. You'll have to find another reckless miss for such adventures," she said, moving out of his embrace before he decided to drag her off into the darkness.

"A pity," he said, sounding as if he meant it. "I hope you remain in London. I would like the opportunity to persuade you to my side."

"Oh, Frost . . . you might not believe me, but I am already on your side," she said, walking away from him. It might be more prudent for her to return to the ballroom without him. "And that's why you are a very dangerous man."

The earl was much like his friend. He would never offer a lady his heart.

Frost shook his head. "Hunter has no idea what he is up against. I can't decide if I pity or envy him."

"I hope you'll allow him to figure things out himself."

"Striving to gain the upper hand, eh?"

"A lady needs to exploit her advantage when challenging a Lord of Vice."

"And clever," he said, suddenly coming to a decision. "Very well, I'll keep my opinions to myself."

"See that you do." She hesitated and glanced back. "And perhaps one day I will reply truthfully to the question you refrained from asking."

"And what question is that, Lady Grace?"

"You want to know whose kisses I prefer—yours or the duke's?"

Frost's shoulders shook as he laughed. "Oh, darling, more to the point, I know whose kisses you prefer this evening. Unless Hunter is an utter fool, I will have to be content with my singular triumph."

Grace was still smiling when she rejoined the fretting Lady Netherley and her companions.

Chapter Eight

Hunter was in a foul mood.

It had taken him minutes to locate Lady Netherley. Unfortunately, the marchioness was not very forthcoming about Lady Grace or her whereabouts. Neither was Sin's wife, Juliana. Or Regan, Isabel, or Sophia when he encountered the ladies. Reign and Dare were distracted with their wives. As for Sin, Hunter assumed he was busy attempting to coax his lady to leave the ball early.

Someone had told him Frost and Vane were in attendance, but he had not seen either gentleman.

How difficult was it to track down one lady?

Annoyed that once again his thoughts were directed toward the chit, he opened the door with more force than was necessary. Hunter stepped into the room. The interior was lit, and appeared to be a small private parlor. Perhaps it had been intended as a respite from the activities below, but no one had taken advantage of the solitude.

"Hunter, this is an unexpected pleasure."

He immediately recognized the feminine voice. Putting a half smile on his face, he turned to greet the one lady he would have avoided if he had known she had decided to attend the Lovelaces' ball. "Lady Cliffton, how long has it been?"

"Too long if you have forgotten that you used to call me Portia," she said, the hint of a pout forming on her full lips.

"That was before you married Cliffton." He took her hand and bowed. "You should be grateful I have decided to behave myself."

The twenty-eight-year-old Portia Fletcher, Countess of Cliffton, looked as lovely as she had when he'd first met her, when she was seventeen and attending her first ball.

A year and a half older than Portia, Hunter had been smitten that first meeting. Three weeks later, he was convinced that he was in love. It had been a unique experience for him, for no other lady had touched his heart as Portia had. Nevertheless, their future appeared bleak from the onset. While the lady's family was determined to see her marry well, Hunter had been unable to offer for her hand.

He had a promise to keep to his grandmother.

No amount of tearful pleas from Portia could persuade him into breaking his vow. Disappointed by his decision and concerned that their daughter's friendship with Hunter might discourage other wealthy suitors, her father accepted the first marriage offer, which happened to be the slightly older Lord Cliffton.

Although Hunter had no right to interfere, he had tried to talk Portia into refusing Cliffton's offer. She was willing as long as Hunter discarded Lady Grace so he could marry her. He had been tempted. At least his feelings for Portia would not have been feigned. In the end, her parents had won. They justly forbade him from seeing their daughter, and then used his abandonment to convince her that Lord Cliffton was a respectable choice after her scandalous behavior with a gentleman who was engaged to marry another lady.

Portia married Cliffton and gave the earl two handsome sons. On the surface, she seemed content with her marriage. Hunter deliberately kept his distance. He had done enough to hurt her and himself. From that day on, he avoided emotional entanglements. His ill-fated relationship with Portia was just another reason why he had resented the young girl his grandmother had foisted off on him. When he had lost Portia, it had felt as if love had been plucked from his grasp.

The passing years and the nameless women who had briefly caught his interest had eased the pain of choosing his honor over love. These days, while he occasionally felt regret, he was also plagued with a lingering guilt over Portia. Not once had he even asked for her forgiveness.

He smiled wistfully. "You look well, my lady. If you were not already married, all the chits hopeful for a good match this season would be envious of your beauty."

"May I return the compliment?" she asked, entering the small parlor. "It has been three years since I last spoke to you. Where have you been hiding yourself that you have no time to visit with old friends?"

He stifled the small annoyance he felt at the suggestion that he had been hiding from her. "I have not been exactly hiding, Portia. I just have other amusements that distract me from spending my evenings in stuffy ballrooms."

Would she be appalled to learn that he enjoyed last season at Madame Venna's Golden Pearl before she closed the doors forever? In many ways, there were very few differences between the ladies of the *ton* and the women he bedded at the brothel. Both of them required payment of some kind.

"For some time, I have longed to speak with you," the countess said, staring at him with a worshipful expression that had once made him feel invincible and capable of heroic feats.

Then he had failed her, and her adoration seemed akin to mockery.

"The Duke of Huntsley is *here*? In this ballroom?"

What confidence she had gained in her flirtatious exchange with Frost swiftly faded with the announcement that the duke had arrived and was currently searching for her.

"I am afraid so, my dear," Lady Netherley said, gazing anxiously at Grace. "I told him you were—" She made a vague gesture with her hand. "About.

Hunter was impatient so he set off to look for you on his own. By the by, where were you? You and Frost seemed to vanish after your dance."

Her cheeks warmed at the implication. "We were just getting to know each other," she said weakly. "He said he was curious about me since the duke rarely speaks of me."

How could he, when he had not bothered to inquire after her?

Now that he had finally come for her, she was uncertain how she felt about it. There was a fluttering in her stomach, and her palms were beginning to sweat.

"Shall I have someone bring the coach to the front door?" Lady Netherley asked, correctly guessing that a part of Grace wanted to flee.

The other part was relieved it was almost over.

"Are you leaving?" Lady Sinclair inquired, likely overhearing the marchioness's question. "I thought you might. It was one of the reasons why I told Sin to keep Hunter away from the ballroom this evening."

Grace glared at Lady Netherley. "You told Juliana, too? How many people are conspiring against me?"

"No one is plotting against you, Grace," Juliana said soothingly. "While I do not quite understand the dowager's intentions for betrothing you to her grandson at such a tender age, I assume it was necessary. Nevertheless, this situation with Hunter is simply unacceptable, and do not believe for one minute that you are to blame."

"I have always thought so," Grace said drily.

"Everyone will tell you that Hunter is a good man. Stubborn, I grant you, and oftentimes selfish, but he never shirks his duties."

"Why are you telling me this?"

"Because I hope you will give him a chance. Us, as well," she said, her gesture encompassing Lady Netherley. "It was one of the reasons why we orchestrated this introduction before you encountered Hunter. We want to show you that you are not alone. You have friends, even if you decide that you do not wish to be the Duchess of Huntsley."

"Frost advised against the match," she blurted out.

Juliana's green eyes hardened, reminding Grace of emeralds. "Of course he did," she muttered, exchanging a look of annoyance with the elderly marchioness. "May I offer you some friendly advice? In the future, walk away from Frost if he begins to share his opinion on the subject of marriage. It will spare you from his ignorance, not to mention a mild headache."

The urge to defend Lord Chillingsworth bubbled up inside her, but it would have taken more time than she had. Besides, it was obvious that this was not the first time the blond marchioness had disagreed with the earl.

"I will alert the servants of our departure," Lady Netherley said, her voice quavering with unspoken emotion.

Grace couldn't decide if she was distressed over

their leaving or the small detail that her evening had not gone as planned.

"No," she said quietly, touching the older woman on the arm to delay her from seeing to her task. "I am staying."

Lady Netherley brightened instantly. "You are?"

Juliana studied Grace's face. "Are you certain? No one was intending to force a meeting this evening." She rolled her eyes as she shook her head. "Hunter came up with this foolish idea on his own."

Her right eyebrow arced in astonishment at the twenty-four-year-old marchioness's uncharitable opinion. According to Lady Netherley, Juliana had married Sin five years ago. Although Sin was not the first Lord of Vice to marry—that honor went to a very young Earl of Rainecourt—Juliana had been the lady to herald the changes that were about to take place within Nox. As the men married, their loyalties subtly shifted from the boyhood bonds they had forged to the new lives they were building with their wives.

"Nineteen years is long enough, do you not agree?" Grace wondered out loud.

Because of her grandfather and the dowager, she was supposed to be the one who would alter the Duke of Huntsley's life. Perhaps she could not blame him for fighting to hold on to the life he had built with his own hands.

"Juliana, do you know where I might find His Grace?"

The young marchioness's lips twitched at Grace's formality, but she tipped her head to convey the direction in which to find the duke. "Across the ballroom, and head for the doors to the outer passageway. You might find him near the staircase."

"Lady Netherley?"

"Yes, dear girl," she said, eager to make amends for her loose tongue. "Do you wish for me to join you?"

"No, but it is kind of you to offer. I thought you might want to alert the servants to prepare for our departure," Grace said, squaring her shoulders. "Something tells me that my meeting with the Duke of Huntsley will be brief."

The anxiety Grace had been feeling seemed a futile exercise when she realized the duke was not in the passageway as Juliana had presumed. Perhaps he had gone upstairs? Her gloved hand brushed the ornately carved newel as she glanced upward and met the amused gaze of Lord Chillingsworth.

"Looking for someone, darling?"

Recalling Juliana's warning, Grace hesitated. Was the earl friend or foe? The question cast his kiss in a sinister light as well. Had Huntsley sent his friend to seduce her?

"So many questions, I see," Frost said, descending to meet her halfway. "And worries. Has someone been whispering naughty tales about me?"

"Not at all!" she said quickly, causing him to chuckle.

"Indeed. I'll let you in on a tiny secret. Whatever you were told was only partly true. My friends and I do try to protect the ladies from some of the unsavory aspects of our lives." Before she could inquire, Frost continued, "By now, you've learned Hunter has escaped his guards and is presently somewhere in this house. Presumably searching for you."

"Ah . . . yes," she said, glancing over the earl's shoulder, but he appeared to be alone. "Do you know the whereabouts of your friend?"

His turquoise-blue eyes shimmered with delight. "Indeed, fair lady, I do. Continue up the staircase, and turn left. There is a small parlor two doors down on the right. You will find him there."

"Thank you," she said, lifting the front of her skirt high enough to avoid stepping on the hem as she ascended the stairs. As she passed Frost, she paused. "Does he know?"

"Know what, Grace?"

She took a breath to steady her nerves. "Is he waiting for me?"

He glanced up and appeared to contemplate her question. "No, darling. Hunter is impatient, which you'll discover for yourself. If you get the opportunity, please send him my regards."

Lord Chillingsworth's enigmatic comment did nothing to ease the butterflies in Grace's stomach.

Her hand briefly connected with the polished oak balustrade as she made her way upstairs to the next landing. She smiled benignly at the couple sitting on the small bench at the top of the stairs. They had slipped away from the noise of the ballroom to share a quiet moment together.

Grace headed left, giving them their privacy. Her gaze found the door almost immediately, and someone had left it open. Perhaps even the Duke of Huntsley. It never occurred to her until now that this was some ruse on Frost's part, a clever excuse to separate her from the other guests.

But for what purpose?

She glanced over her shoulder, but he had not followed. He was still at his post on the stairs, or he had strolled off to join his friends. She started to cross the threshold of the parlor, but what she glimpsed within the interior of the room caused her to halt. With her legs abruptly locked in place, she used her hand to prevent herself from losing her balance.

The Duke of Huntsley was there. Nor was he alone. A dark-haired woman had managed to coil herself around him like a common vine her gardeners ripped out of the colorful flower beds by the roots.

"This isn't the place, Portia," the duke murmured, doing nothing to untangle himself from what appeared to be a torrid embrace. He had even placed his hand on the lady's back to hold her in place.

"Then when? I must see you," the woman pleaded, her breasts deliberately pressing against his chest.

Leave before you are caught.

Grace commanded her limbs to move, but she seemed frozen in place. Was this woman the duke's mistress? One of her neighbors had trouble with his wife when the unfortunate lady discovered that her husband had been keeping a mistress. Her friends told her that all gentlemen kept mistresses. The notion disturbed her sleep for weeks. All the while, she had wondered if the Duke of Huntsley had taken mistresses. He was certainly wealthy enough to keep one. Then her uncle confirmed her suspicions on one of his visits. According to him, her betrothed had an entire stable of fallen women for his pleasure.

Was this the reason why Frost had directed her upstairs? Had he wanted to prove to her that the duke was unwilling to commit himself to just one lady?

If so, the message had been delivered like a blade into her heart.

The Duke of Huntsley's gaze shifted from his companion's face to Grace. "We are not alone."

His warning was as effective as a bucket of frigid water. The woman stiffened, immediately releasing the duke. In one graceful movement she slipped out of his arms and turned to confront Grace.

"Forgive me," Grace said, her fingers digging into the door frame. "I did not mean to intrude. I was told that the parlor was empty."

It was a lie, but she would do anything to leave with her dignity intact. Then she was going to seek out Frost and deliver the slap he sorely deserved for tricking her.

The duke's gaze glinted with recognition and pleasure. "It is you. How unexpected. It appears fate does have a sense of humor. Please, you are welcome to join us." He gave the woman a pointed glance. "Though I doubt Portia can remain. Were you not telling me that you had to rejoin your husband?"

His mistress was married?

The woman's mouth thinned with displeasure. She clearly did not like to be dismissed. Or perhaps, she was not happy leaving her lover in the company of another woman.

"Yes . . . yes, of course," she said, her movements as stiff as her voice. "We can discuss this at a later date."

"Please send my regards to your husband, Portia."

The woman nodded. As she walked toward Grace, she delivered a scathing look. It was enough to prompt her to move out of the lady's way. This mysterious Portia was not the only lady who hoped to make a quick escape.

"Oh, I have no intention of letting you leave . . . not when I had hoped we would encounter each other again," he said, extending his hand in a sweeping motion toward one of the sofas. "Please. Sit."

"It might be for the best if I leave."

The duke smiled with a confidence that made Grace grind her molars. "Not for me. I thought I might have to bribe every coachman in London to discover your whereabouts."

"Why would you want to do that?"

Her unfriendly tone managed to startle him. "You never gave me a chance to introduce myself."

"An introduction is unnecessary. I fear, your reputation precedes you. You are Nicolas Stuart Towers, Duke of Huntsley."

Grace almost ruined her cool announcement by grinning at his look of astonishment. Oh, he had not been expecting her to know his name.

Granted, he recovered from his shock rather swiftly. "Who told you?" he harshly demanded.

"Why do you believe someone told me your name?" she asked, feigning puzzlement. "After all, I was exploring the market when you stumbled across me and my servants."

"Do I know you?"

"No," she replied, confident that he could detect her sincerity. One thing was certain. The Duke of Huntsley did not know her at all. "As I said, you have a rather notorious reputation. Your Portia is proof that the rumors about you were not exaggerations."

Whether or not she agreed with his method, Frost had done her a favor. Before she left town, she might even thank him for it.

"Portia doesn't belong to me," he said, his voice

edged with annoyance. "We are old friends. She is married to Lord Cliffton."

Grace glanced away. She had been introduced to Lord Cliffton. He was an older gentleman who appeared to be in his early fifties. She wondered if he suspected that his wife was in love with another man.

"I see. Well, I have tarried too long and should return to my friends." She hoped Lady Netherley's coach was waiting for them just beyond the front door. "Enjoy the rest of your evening."

The duke was at her side before she could take a single step.

"You're slippery, but I don't mind putting my hands on you," he said, proving it by grabbing both of her wrists.

"Release me" was her haughty reply.

He lowered his head until they were nose-to-nose. "Give me one good reason why I should."

Oh, she had one guaranteed to ruin his evening.

Her upper lip curled into a sneer. "My name is Lady Grace Kearly. And I am the last woman in London you want to be touching."

Huntsley released her as if her flesh had burned him.

It was the final insult. "I thought so." She expelled her breath with a soft huffing noise, pivoted, and walked away before she did something truly outrageous.

"Grace!"

He roared her name, but she had no intention of

sticking around to find out why he sounded so furious. Why was he angry at her? She was the one who had caught him fondling another woman.

A *married* woman!

She shivered in disgust. Ugh, and he had touched her. When she returned home, she would have to order a bath so she could scrub the filth of him from her body.

"Do not take another step!"

Grace had already reached the stairs. "I have nothing more to say to you!" she shouted back, startling the couple who were sitting on the bench.

Her skirt limited her pace, but she made her way down the steps as swiftly as she could. She was not surprised to see Frost leaning against the balustrade where she had left him.

"Trouble, darling?"

"I am not talking to you, either!" she said, not bothering to stop. She would deal with Frost later. Or worse, she would allow Juliana to mete out the punishment he richly deserved.

"Darling?" Hunter echoed his friend's false endearment. "How long have you known Frost?"

Although he did not deserve an answer, Grace whirled around and gave one to him anyway. "Long enough for him to kiss me in the garden."

There. It was the least both of them deserved for embarrassing her.

In the distance, she could hear the duke growl, "You kissed her!"

She did not linger to hear Frost's reply. If there was any justice, Huntsley would knock some of the arrogance out of the earl.

Both men had played her for a fool.

Grace realized she was muttering to herself when Regan's face came into focus as she blocked the way. Standing beside her was a tall gentleman with light blond hair and blue-gray eyes. The man was likely her husband, though everything was not as it seemed in London.

"What happened?" Regan demanded, glancing at the man for support. "Did you find Hunter?"

"Oh, I found him," Grace managed to say between clenched teeth. "Where is Lady Netherley?"

She had to leave this house.

Grace was prepared to walk if necessary.

Regan frowned. "She is outdoors, waiting in the coach. Can you tell me what happened?"

She shook her head. "Another time. I—"

"Lady Grace Kearly, I am far from finished with you!" the duke shouted over the din of the ballroom, which abruptly quieted at his outrageous declaration.

Regan and her husband audibly gasped. Grace cringed. Thanks to the horrid man, the gossips would be speculating on what she and the duke had been doing outside the ballroom.

"If you have any affection for Huntsley, you will detain him so I can take my leave," she whispered to the couple. "Otherwise I cannot be accountable for my actions."

Regan briskly nodded. "Go."

Grace did not need a second invitation. She fled the ballroom, trusting her new friends to calm the irate duke.

Chapter Nine

She did not cry on the drive home.

Nor was she waiting for the fussing Lady Netherley to depart before she succumbed to her tears. While Rosemary and the marchioness mumbled excuses about preparing some tea, in truth, they were talking about what had happened this evening.

For the first time, the Duke of Huntsley saw *her*.

It was not the romantic encounter she had dreamed of as a child. Nor was it the chillingly polite introduction she had practiced in front of her looking glass.

Alone in the drawing room, she had managed to curl up into a small ball at the end of the sofa with her knees brought up to her chest. She was exposing an indecent amount of leg, but there was no one to witness her careless pose of misery.

There had been revulsion in his expression.

Grace closed her eyes in an attempt to banish the image from her brain. His reaction had cut her to the quick, but how could she expect anything more from a man who took married women for mistresses?

A soft sound of disgust was expelled as she exhaled. It was not for the duke, but for herself.

She should have demanded her freedom years ago.

In the distance, someone was pounding on the door. It was probably Lady Netherley's coachman inquiring after her. She had insisted on returning with her. The poor lady blamed herself for the debacle this evening.

There were voices in the hall. The coachman, Grace thought. Although she could not overhear what was being discussed, it sounded as if the marchioness was reluctant to leave. She lifted her cheek from her forearm and tilted her head to listen. Instead of feeling sorry for herself, she should go out into the hall and assure everyone that she was fine.

Before she could straighten, the double doors burst open and the Duke of Huntsley was striding into the drawing room.

"Forgive me, my lady," Rosemary said, her eyes burning with indignation. "His Grace insisted on seeing you."

Grace straightened, allowing her bare feet to touch the rug as she sat up. The proper thing would have been to stand and greet the duke with a curtsy. However, the man had entered her residence after midnight. She was too tired to be respectful or polite.

Lady Netherley entered the room, leaning heavily on her walking stick. "Hunter, be sensible. This is not the hour to be calling on—"

"We are betrothed," he said, towering over her.

Perhaps it would have been more prudent to stand. "And I do not give a damn what anyone thinks. Leave us."

"My lady?"

Grace refused to place Rosemary in an awkward position. If she was disrespectful to the duke, he might sack her, and she could not bear losing her dear friend.

"I will be fine," she said, unable to keep the tremor from her voice. She cleared her throat. "It's late. Lady Netherley, I have kept you from your bed. With your permission, Rosemary will summon your coachman and he will see you home."

Lady Netherley seemed reluctant to leave her in the duke's care. She also appeared to be sorely vexed at the man she thought of as a son. "Hunter."

"I think you have done enough this evening, Lady Netherley," he said coldly.

At the elderly woman's gasp, the duke scowled at Grace—as if she were responsible for his harsh outburst—then shoved his hand through his hair. "Forgive me, Lady Netherley. It is not my intention to lash you with my temper. Go home. You have known me for most of my life. No harm will come to Grace. You have my word on it."

Grace was not convinced, but his words appeared to mollify Lady Netherley.

"Very well." She sighed. "However, I expect to see you tomorrow afternoon in my drawing room. I wish to discuss your recent actions and propensity to be—oh, what is the phrase my son has often used of late—yes, a boorish arse."

To her amazement, the duke winced and gave the marchioness an apologetic look. "I will be happy to call on you, my lady."

"See that you do," Lady Netherley said crisply. "Grace, I will leave you my walking stick, if you require it."

"I do not believe that will be necessary, my lady." If she needed to defend her virtue, there was enough marble and pottery on hand to crack a man's skull.

Guessing the lady's thoughts, the Duke of Huntsley's gaze narrowed.

"Good evening, then." Lady Netherley took her leave.

Rosemary glared at the duke's back. "I have polishing to do just beyond the door. If you need anything, my lady, just call out my name."

"Thank you, Rosemary."

Huntsley glanced at the doors after Rosemary shut them. "She polishes silver in the middle of the night?"

Grace shrugged. "I suppose it's as plausible as you desiring a congenial conversation after you bullied your way into my residence."

He jammed his fists into his hips and stared down at her. "Nineteen years have passed, and my opinion hasn't changed. You were put on this earth to torment me, Lady Grace Kearley."

* * *

Grace might have been sitting, but she did not have a submissive bone in her slender body. Dry-eyed, she stared up at him with defiance and something else he couldn't quite define.

"What a dreadful thing to say!" She pointed a finger at him. "Not five minutes in my presence and you lose all civility."

"You would provoke the devil himself to violence," he grumbled, walking to the table against the wall and picking up the oil lamp.

"What are you about, Your Grace?"

"As my betrothed, you are permitted to call me Huntsley, though I prefer Hunter." He placed the lamp on the table next to the sofa. "As to what I am doing . . . I thought it was obvious. You dashed out of the Lovelaces' house so quickly I never got a good look at you."

"Why are you suddenly curious? You've had nineteen years to study me and could not be troubled to send me a single letter."

Unhappy with the sudden brightness, Grace shifted a few inches away from the end of the sofa. He thought about sitting next to her on the sofa. It would be the easiest way to make certain she remained seated. Instead, he chose one of the chairs directly across from her. It bordered on rudeness, but he wanted an unfettered perusal of this woman.

"You were a beautiful child," he said absently. "My grandmother predicted your beauty would garner the envy of queens."

"And what would she say of you, Your Grace?"

"Hunter."

She ignored his prompting. "If she were alive, would she be proud of the man you have become?"

Hunter might have been angry when he had arrived, but her efforts to provoke him were amusing. She assumed erroneously that he had little control of his emotions. On the contrary, he excelled at tethering his feelings. He prided himself in his ability to not allow his emotion to rule his actions. If he did not, Grace's rash attempt to incite a fight between him and Frost by claiming that his friend had kissed her might have succeeded.

Jealousy was one emotion he had never experienced, and refused to indulge.

All those years ago, when Portia told him that she had planned to marry Cliffton, it was guilt and sadness that had driven him to plead with her to reconsider. At her refusal, he had buried even those feelings under layers of icy control.

His control served him well when dealing with women. Unfortunately for them, he could not be manipulated as easily as other men. He also could walk away when a lover grew tiresome. No anger or guilt.

Or that had been the case until the lady who had caught his interest had blurted out her name. It surprised him that his initial reaction was a feeling of betrayal. How could this beautiful lady be the one woman he had rejected years ago? The next emotion to bubble through the cracks of his control was anger.

Hunter did not want to be attracted to the lady his grandmother had handpicked for him. He also sensed that Grace was equally unsettled by his proximity.

If Dare and Sin had not held him back after Grace's hasty departure, Hunter was still unsure what he might have done had he caught up to her before she reached Lady Netherley's coach.

Paddling her backside was the least she deserved.

Although his friends begged him not to follow their coach, he ignored their sound advice, telling himself that the ladies needed his protection while they traveled the streets of London.

As he prepared to knock on the front door, he had convinced himself that he was doing her a favor by confronting her. He had envisioned the poor girl sobbing in the marchioness's arms.

However, the lady staring back at him had clearly not shed a single tear. According to Regan and the others, Grace was eager to sever all ties to him. If she had put her request into a letter, he would have considered accepting her offer.

Then he would have politely declined her request.

She did not understand that the vow he made extended beyond her protection. His honor and sense of duty was bound to the contract—as was the lady herself.

In time, Grace would understand her decision to travel to London only hurled them to the inevitable.

She would marry him.

Grace deliberately crossed her eyes, pulling him

away from his thoughts. "You were content to never inquire about me to see what became of the girl you were entrusted with. Now you are staring at me as if you can somehow recover those lost years. It is a futile endeavor."

"True." Hunter had visited Frethwell Hall, but it was obvious no one had told her. He had regrets, but he had kept his promise to his grandmother. Lady Grace had been raised according to her station in life, and had never lacked for anything. His only failing as far as he was concerned was that he had selfishly put aside too many years for himself.

"Then what do you propose we do?" she demanded, growing frustrated by his silence.

Now that he had met her, there was only one thing he could do to make amends for his absence and keep his honor intact.

"I propose we get married."

"No," she said, her soft denial was reinforced with an iron will. How many years had she longed to hear him speak those very words?

Too many.

Grace had plotted her own course. With Porter's assistance, she would figure out a way to free both herself and Huntsley.

Instead of anger, he sat back in his chair. He clasped his large hands together as his fingers tapped in a contemplative gesture.

"Why?"

Surprised by the question, she made a wordless sputtering noise. "Why? I can give you nineteen reasons, Your Grace. Let me ask you—how many years would I have continued to wait if there wasn't a stipulation in that awful contract that we had to be wedded by my twenty-first birthday?"

He remained silent.

"I thought so," she said, her right hand curling into a fist. She had never struck anyone in her life, but she might make an exception for this arrogant man. "If you had your way, I would still be waiting for you at Frethwell Hall. Here and now. Tomorrow. Next year, and the years that followed."

His lips twitched. "Impossible. You must have missed the part where I am to get you with child within eighteen months of the marriage. My grandmother liked to have her way, and she was a stickler for details."

Grace realized her mouth had fallen open and swiftly closed it. Why had no one pointed out that particular clause? Of course he would require an heir from her. She just had not expected to become a brood mare so quickly. How long would it take for him to get her with child? She could be sent back to Frethwell Hall weeks after their marriage.

"Grace," he said, oblivious to her tumultuous thoughts. "It was never my intention to allow so many years to pass without visiting you. I realize this is not the most auspicious beginning, but I have faith we can set things right. You are not quite one-and-twenty, and I am prepared to honor my end of the bargain. We will marry as soon as I can obtain a special license and—"

"No."

It took a few seconds for her rejection to register on his face. Grace concluded that not many people refused the duke. "I beg your pardon."

"Was I not succinct?" she asked, wiggling her toes and recalling that she was barefoot. "Or perhaps I spoke too softly."

"No, I heard you," he said in clipped tones. "I just expect you to look me in the eye when you are tossing away an arrangement that was created for your benefit."

To prove that she not intimidated by his presence, she lifted her eyes until she was staring into his amber gaze. The brilliant color blazed like twin suns. "Let's not forget that you have benefited from this arrangement as well. Porter has told me that your investments have made us both very rich, and no doubt your liberties with my assets gave you certain advantages over the years."

"It is kind of you to acknowledge that I have made you very wealthy. Most orphans would be grateful to be called an heiress."

What sort of man could be cruel enough to remind her that she was all alone in this world? "I also happen to be the daughter of a duke," she said evenly. "Nor am I a fool, Your Grace. I will soon be of age, and will no longer require you to be my guardian. The duty did not suit you, and I, for one, am grateful it has come to an end."

Seconds later he had her pinned in place by blocking any means to escape with his muscular arms. He had moved so swiftly, she could not fathom how he had done it.

"I am much more than your guardian, Lady Grace," he said, his close proximity forcing her to tip her head back so she could meet his furious gaze. "I am your husband."

"No yet," she said triumphantly. "Not ever, if I have a say about it."

"The only words I require from you are *yes* and *I do*," he purred, his body filling her vision. The subtle scent of man with the hint of lavender filled her nose.

"Words you may hear often from your servants and mistresses, but you will not hear them from me."

She placed her palms against his chest. Even through the layers of his evening coat, waistcoat, and linen shirt, she could feel the heat of his body. It struck her that this was the first time she had truly touched him, and the intimacy of the gesture unsettled her. "If you are the gentleman you are purported to be, you will step away and leave this house." She pushed against his chest, but it was as solid as a wall.

The duke leaned closer. "Or else, what?"

"Or else, I will call for Rosemary," she replied, frantically grasping for the first weapon that came to mind. His nearness was scattering her wits. "She will wake the rest of the staff, or summon the watch. I do not care if she wakes everyone in this square. As much as I have enjoyed this little visit, you have over-stayed your welcome and I wish for you to leave."

His lips were scant inches from hers. "Perhaps I could persuade you to change your mind."

Was he planning to kiss her until she begged him to stay?

Grace felt her face growing hot at the thought.

"You have had nineteen years to sway me, Your Grace," she said in a quavering voice. "And you have succeeded. I no longer desire to marry you, and I want you to leave."

She held her breath as she awaited his reply.

"Very well." The Duke of Huntsley surprised her by yielding to her demand. He straightened and ad-justed his sleeves. "I can see that I should have scru-tinized the various governesses and tutors that Porter employed over the years. Clearly, respect, gratitude, and obedience were stricken from your lessons."

"Respect and gratitude are not summoned on command, Your Grace. They are earned. As for obedience—" She daintily shrugged. "I have never been particularly obedient. Just view it as one more reason why you wish to tear up this marriage con-tract as eagerly as I do."

She expected the duke to be difficult. Perhaps even utter a few threats to ruin any thought of sleep. Instead he chuckled and shook his head. "You are not what I expected, Lady Grace."

"Neither are you."

He grimaced, but accepted the insult, knowing it was deserved. "Before I depart under your Rosemary's watchful eye, I feel it necessary to tell you a few things about myself."

"I know enough."

"No, my lady, you don't." He sobered, and she felt the full impact of his amber gaze. "I gave my word to your grandfather and my grandmother that I would marry you when you came of age."

"Both of them died a long time ago. No one will think less of you for disappearing for a few more weeks. By then, I will be twenty-one and the contract will no longer be a concern."

"*I* will think less of me," he said, opening the door. Just beyond the doorway, Rosemary scurried out of sight. "I gave my word and we will adhere to the terms, even if we find the situation unpalatable."

Grace chased after him. "But—"

He paused, waiting for Rosemary to rush forward and open the door. Grace halted to maintain a safe distance between them.

"One more thing. I suggest you begin to think of me less as your benevolent guardian, and more as your husband. You will discover I will be more attentive in this new stage of our relationship." He inclined his head. "Sleep well, Duchess."

The Duke of Huntsley departed, leaving both women to stare speechlessly as he disappeared into the night

Chapter Ten

Grace wondered if she would ever get used to town life.

London never seemed to sleep. Throughout the night, she could hear the sounds of horses pulling their varying conveyances up and down the street. The robust voices of the coachmen, pedestrians, and the watchman drifted up to her window. After Hunter's visit it had taken her hours to drift off to sleep. When she did, Grace was startled out of her restless sleep by a woman's shriek. She slipped out of bed and warily approached the window. The cry of distress quickly dissolved into throaty giggles as the woman's two male companions escorted her down the street and away from her curious gaze.

By the time Rosemary entered the bedchamber to wake her, Grace felt as if she had only been asleep for a few hours. Despite this, the excitement of London had yet to diminish. As unpleasant as last evening had been, encountering Hunter had been necessary. It had spurred her to call on Mr. Porter.

Regrettably he had not been in his office. His rude assistant told her that she needed an appointment and there were no exceptions to the rule. Disheartened by this news, she went ahead and scheduled a meeting for the following week.

To cheer her up, Rosemary suggested that they visit Covent Gardens before they headed back to the town house they were renting for some tea.

"I hear they have pineapples," Rosemary said enthusiastically.

Grace smiled, since pineapples were not often served at Frethwell. "If so, then we should buy one. Or two, if you wish."

"I vow I could eat a dozen in a week," the woman responded, chuckling at the outlandish boast. "Just hold on to your reticule. There are pickpockets and cheats all around us."

Grace shyly nodded to two ladies who passed by them close enough to brush her elbow. "Your confidence in your fellow man astounds me."

Rosemary frowned at a well-dressed man who stepped in front of her. "If you please, my good man. I have my lady to see to without you barring my way." A few steps later, she caught up to Grace. "Well, my dear, I am too poor to afford to be confident. Besides, you have enough in you for both of us."

"Oh, you do not fool me, Miss Shaw," Grace said, her eyes widening as she noticed a man with a small monkey on his shoulder. "I seem to recall the year three governesses declared me too stubborn to instruct and departed with very little notice. You said—"

"The uppity chits held no challenge for an intellectual lady," the woman finished, her expression revealing it was a fond memory for her as well.

"See? Ever the optimist." Grace turned left and headed for the man with the monkey.

"I thought we were picking up a pineapple?"

"A brief diversion," she said over her shoulder, confident Rosemary would follow. "My, my . . . what a handsome beast you are," she praised, utterly enchanted with the little monkey.

Hunter had just finished paying for several bouquets of flowers when the bemusing observation reached his ears. At first, he thought the woman was speaking to him, but a quick glance caused him to do a double take as he realized that he knew the lady. Nor was he pleased to see her wandering about Covent Garden without a proper escort. As he contemplated his next moves, Lady Grace was unaware that she was being observed. Her attention was centered on the elderly gentleman and his exotic pet.

The florist handed Hunter two bouquets wrapped in paper to protect the delicate petals. "Will there be anything else, Your Grace?"

"No, these will suffice, Allie," he said, laying the bundles over his arm. He and his servants had been conducting business with the middle-aged woman for more than ten years.

"Courting only two ladies this week?" Her smile revealed a missing bottom tooth. "They must be wearing you down."

"Not a chance." He leaned over and kissed her on a cheek weathered by age and sun. "I'm just waiting for you to get tired of that old husband of yours."

"Go on with ye." She chuckled and waved him off, delighted by his teasing. "I don't melt as effortlessly as those hothouse blooms you fancy gents prefer."

"Let me know if you want me to change your mind, Allie."

Hunter cast a curious eye toward Lady Grace as she chatted with the old gentleman. She looked like a hothouse bloom cast in a field of weeds. From his position, he noted that she had one servant at her side. It wasn't enough for the future Duchess of Huntsley. Lady Grace should be surrounded by a dozen servants.

Attired in a white round dress of India muslin that was decorated with multiple rows of flounces at the bottom of the skirt, she wore an open spencer fashioned from rose-lavender-colored satin. Braided cording drew the observer's eye to her shoulders and the soft curves of her breasts.

He had planned to call on Saint and Catherine this afternoon. Afterward, he was planning to surprise Vane's mother with a brief visit so he could apologize for his boorish behavior last evening. He had no time for courtship, but he had no intention of leaving her alone. Hunter strolled toward her.

The high emotions of last evening had not allowed him to appreciate Lady Grace's beauty. His earlier assessments were faint praise. The young lady was truly exquisite. Green eyes, unblemished fair skin that glowed with vitality, a nose and chin that could not be improved upon by the greatest sculptors of the world, and limbs that moved as gracefully as a dancer's. In the sunlight, the curls that were nestled beneath her bonnet—white satin trimmed with rose-lavender and white feathers—gleamed like gold threads. She represented everything pure and innocent, while he had spent their time apart immersing himself in debauchery.

He had been right to stay away from her. Otherwise, he might have been tempted to turn her into a woman before nature had finished molding her into the glorious creature she had become.

Lady Grace had noticed him as well. The young woman abruptly grew silent, and her shoulders stiffened at his approach. The female servant had noticed him, too. She moved in front of her charge before he had reached them.

"Good afternoon, ladies," Hunter said, cradling his flower bouquets in his left arm while he tipped his hat and bowed. "I see you have a fondness for beasts."

Lady Grace stared blankly at him. "I—I beg your pardon?"

His confidence rose in the face of her befuddled state. He often had this effect on young ladies, which

was one of the reasons why he tried to avoid ballrooms and matchmakers. Normally, he just excused
himself and headed for the nearest card room or sent
his apologies to his host before his hasty departure.
For some reason, it pleased him that his presence
muddled his duchess's tongue.

"I was referring to the monkey." To the owner,
Hunter asked, "Does the creature bite?"

"Only those he doesn't like, milord," was the man's
hoarse reply. He reached into a pocket and retrieved
a small nut. "As I was saying, would you care to feed
him, miss?"

The question gave her an excuse to dismiss him.
"Yes. Yes, I would, if you do not mind."

Hunter liked the sound of her voice. It did not have
the nasal quality that his last mistress had. Those
melodious tones carried a hint of sophistication that
seemed at odds with her youth.

The man with the monkey placed a small nut in
her gloved hand. "Mind? The rascal practically begs
me for a treat every few minutes. You will be doing
me a favor if you feed him for me."

The man winked at Hunter, inviting him to share
in the jest. He concluded that this was not the first
pretty lady his pet had lured to his side.

Lady Grace glanced warily at the monkey, who
was staring at the nut between her fingers with keen
interest. The beast knew what came next, and he was
literally bobbing up and down with excitement.

"Have a care, my girl," her female companion murmured, not wanting to startle the animal into biting her charge.

"Here you go, little one," Lady Grace said as she held up her offering. "Is this what you want?"

The monkey moved quickly and plucked the nut from her fingers. Startled by its speed, she gasped. The sound caused the animal to jump over the old man's head to land on the opposite shoulder.

Believing it was a trick, several people around them applauded. Lady Grace reddened in embarrassment as her chaperone laughed.

"I suspect the beast is more frightened of you than you are of him."

She wrinkled her nose and smiled. "I suppose so."

As if to prove the chaperone wrong, the monkey jumped again, this time leaping onto Lady Grace's slender shoulder. She took a step back to balance her stance, but her composure was remarkable. Most ladies would have been screaming their heads off by now.

"I see he likes you." The old man grinned at her. He did not make any attempt to retrieve his pet.

The monkey indeed seemed to be enjoying his new perch. It sniffed her bonnet and took a tentative bite. Satisfied it was inedible, it circled once before clapping its tiny paws together.

"Is he . . . does he want another nut?" Lady Grace asked, turning her face away to avoid being scratched.

Her servant was less polite about the situation. "Do not just stand there. Retrieve your filthy beast before it gives my lady fleas!"

"Tom does not have fleas!" the owner yelled back. "He likes to play in his bath."

"You named your monkey Tom? What a ridiculous name." For no reason at all, Hunter found the notion hilarious. And then the second admission sank in. "Uh, Tom takes baths with you?"

The old man gave Hunter a withering look. "Not always. He often insists on taking one on his own."

Hunter and several other men could not contain their laughter. Meanwhile, Tom had definitely taken a liking to his new friend. The creature had curled its tail around the blonde's neck as it inspected the decorations on her bonnet.

"He's a marvelous beast," the young woman said, infusing enough cheer that Hunter almost believed her if she did not have a small animal eating her hat. "Perhaps you should take him, good sir. I do not wish to frighten him."

"Do not fret, little miss. Tom is a good judge of character," the owner assured her.

Hunter decided to step in and rescue his brave lady. "With your permission?"

Green eyes as mysterious as a warm sea met his. "Please" was her faint reply.

Hunter merely grunted, pushing his wrapped bouquets into a stranger's hands. "Hold this." He gently untangled the monkey from its lovely perch. Both the animal and its owner chattered at him, but he ignored them. "There, there . . . almost done." He handed the excited animal back to its owner. "Your beast is unharmed."

The elderly man dug into his pocket for a nut. "Here you go, Tom. I have plenty more."

"You're lucky my lady wasn't bitten." The fire was back in the dragon's eyes and mouth.

"Rosemary, please."

Hunter was impressed that Lady Grace had managed to silence the angry woman with her soft plea.

She adjusted her bonnet and smiled at the man. "Thank you and Tom for an interesting afternoon. I have never touched a monkey before, and it was quite an experience. Good day, gentlemen." With a glance, she indicated to her servant that she was ready to depart.

"And good day to you, young miss," the old man called after her. "Come visit Tom again." He glared at Hunter and gave his pet an affectionate pat.

Tom quietly chewed his nut.

Hunter's gaze shifted back to Lady Grace, who seemed determined to disappear into the crowd without bothering to thank him for his part in rescuing her from that damn monkey. With a muttered curse on his lips, he collected his wrapped flowers and chased after the young woman and her servant.

Chapter Eleven

"Slow down," Rosemary said, a slight catch in her breath. "It isn't healthy to be rushing like this."

Grace ignored her companion's order as both her head and heart were racing. She could not believe what had just occurred. Had Hunter been following them? And then there was the monkey—could her awkward predicament have been any more humiliating? "If you wish to purchase those pineapples, we must hurry. At this time of day, there might not be any left."

"In a rush, are we?" Hunter asked with an easy smile. He carried several bundles of what looked to be flowers in the crook of his left arm, and he slowed his pace as he closed the distance between them. "I hope the monkey did not frighten you off."

Oh, he was a handsome scoundrel. Dangerous, too, she mused, noting the thick muscle covering his limbs. He towered over her and Rosemary, and she guessed his height to be slightly over six feet. However, it was his eyes that Grace first noticed. They were a light brown, and in the sunlight the color reminded her of a chunk of amber that was collecting dust in the library of Frethwell Hall. The shade was truly remarkable, and with his thick black eyelashes his gaze could indeed seduce a lady.

"It seemed best to take my leave before the beast devoured the rest of my bonnet," she said, striving for practicality with a hint of humor.

Rosemary gave her an odd glance but said nothing. Grace did not blame her. Her voice sounded strange even to her ears. She could not explain her reaction to the duke's proximity.

"Forgive me if I did not thank you properly," she continued. "I did not mean to be rude, but we have several other calls to make this afternoon."

A light breeze teased the bluntly cut ends of his hair that brushed against the line of his jaw. The color was a rich black without a hint of silver. How old was Hunter? He had been twelve when his grandmother had announced their betrothal. That meant he was slightly older than thirty. A seasoned gentleman, as Rosemary often remarked.

"I understand."

He gave her an appraising look and grinned. Had he noticed that she had been staring? Of course he had. He was probably used to ladies gazing adoringly up into his beautiful amber eyes.

Grace shifted her gaze so she was staring at his shoulder. She could not get into much trouble admiring his frock coat. "I should not have stopped to admire the monkey. I just had never seen a living one before."

His eyebrows came together in puzzlement. "Living?"

"She is referring to taxidermy, Your Grace," Rosemary explained. "One of our neighbors has a house filled with a menagerie of stuffed beasts. Some natural and others not quite."

Hunter appeared fascinated. "Not quite what, dear lady?"

"As God intended," her companion replied, her eyes rolling heavenward as if waiting for *his* opinion on the subject.

Before Hunter could ask her to elaborate further, Grace interjected, "My neighbor has a sense of humor. And an artist's touch when he works on his creations."

"Abominations are more like it."

Grace glared at her friend. "We will have none of that. Not everyone appreciates Arthur's work."

"Arthur?"

Grace took a fortifying breath before she raised her head to face the amusement in his gaze. "My neighbor," she clarified.

Sensing her curiosity on why he appeared to be following her, Hunter got down to business. "I do not make a habit of chasing after beautiful young ladies—"

Grace exchanged knowing glances with Rosemary at the obvious falsehood.

"And I have appointments, as well," he said, his features darkening when he stared down at the wrapped bouquets. "Or did. These are for you."

He filled her arms with the flowers he had purchased. *Probably for another lady,* she thought furiously as she fought back the urge to toss them to the ground and stomp on them.

Before she did anything un-lady-like, she handed the bouquets to Rosemary.

"I feel inclined after your mishap with the monkey to invite you and your companions for some refreshments."

An invitation to tea was the last thing she expected from Hunter. "A generous invitation. However, I—"

"Have appointments," he replied, sounding irritated. "I heard you the first time. Nevertheless, you and I have much to discuss. I had planned on calling on you later to discuss our upcoming marriage, but that is—"

"Completely unnecessary," she put in sharply. "And I must regretfully decline. I am woefully late, and must excuse myself." Grace curtsied. "Again, you have my gratitude for your timely rescue. Good day, Your Grace."

"I have not finished with you, my lady."

Grace might not be familiar with all of Hunter's moods, but she had been around enough gentlemen to recognize that particular tone most men adopted when they were about to lose their temper.

"What you fail to understand, Your Grace, is the unpleasant fact that I am finished with you." She nodded briskly. "Again, I wish you a good day."

She grabbed Rosemary by the arm before the woman could protest, and they continued down the walkway. Their groom trailed after them, carrying their purchases.

"Well, that was extremely rude of you," Rosemary huffed. "The gentleman was kindly inviting us to share a table with him."

"That *gentleman*," Grace said, enunciating every syllable. "Is the Duke of Huntsley!"

Rosemary abruptly halted and gaped in feigned astonishment at her mistress. "A fine time to tell me. I was considering whether to keep him for myself!"

"Oh, you can have him," Grace replied tartly. "Undoubtedly, His Grace has not allowed anything as trivial as a betrothal to prevent him from flirting with every female in London."

Hunter did not pursue Lady Grace, who seemed so determined to escape his company. If he caught up to her, he would have been tempted to paddle her backside to relieve some of the frustration he was feeling.

Or kiss her.

Hunter shook his head to rid himself of the thought. No, the spirited chit needed a firm hand. Kissing Lady Grace would only lead to trouble.

Not that Hunter didn't enjoy playing with fire.

He often sought out danger. It was one of many things he and his friends had in common. It was with some reluctance that he turned his back on the lady and her servants and retraced his steps to find his coach. Despite his initial concerns that Lady Grace needed more servants, he was satisfied that the pair she had retained would see to it that she got home safely.

An hour later, he arrived on the door step of the Sainthill residence. Over the years, he and Saint had formed a deeper bond of friendship, which he supposed was natural considering how much they had in common. Both of them were essentially orphaned at an early age. After his grandmother died, Hunter had eschewed his distant cousins. While the dowager tolerated the greedy sycophants, he had little patience for them. Saint, on the other hand, had been abandoned by his mother after the sudden death of his father. She had gone on to remarry and bear other children, but Saint was not welcome in the new family she had built with her second husband.

Not that Saint gave a damn.

Before he met his wife, Saint had been content to be alone. Hunter had felt the same way, and they had passed many evenings together while the other Lords of Vice sacrificed their freedom for the marriage bed.

Willing or not, you're next, gent.

Hunter ignored the taunt that whispered in his ear.

"Hunter," Catherine said, smiling with open friendliness and affection. "What a pleasant surprise! I just sent one of the servants to fetch Saint. How are you?"

"I am well." He had purchased a bouquet of roses, larkspurs, anemones, and tulips to apologize for interrupting the couple's afternoon, but he had given it away to Lady Grace. "I went to the market and bought you flowers. However, I lost them along the way."

"How very careless of you," Catherine teased. "But I hope you know you are welcome in our home with or without flowers. Saint and I consider you family."

She touched him briefly on the arm, and then was distracted by the servant who had entered the room to announce that Saint would be joining them shortly.

Catherine's words warmed him. Hunter took a moment to study his friend's wife as she gave the servant instructions. The new Marchioness of Sainthill was exquisite with her golden hair arranged into a riot of curls. Her dress was the height of fashion, and the large emerald surrounded by twelve rose-cut diamonds on her left hand signified Saint's love and fidelity to his lady.

The *ton* knew her as Lord Greenshield's natural daughter and the lady who had tamed Sainthill's wild heart. Most would not believe him even if he were cruel enough to speak the truth—the marchioness had once beguiled the males in London as Madame Venna. Hunter saw nothing of the masked proprietress in the serene, confident Catherine. Along with her half-mask and exotic accent, she had cast aside her anger toward the parents who had abandoned her and her need for revenge against those who had hurt her when she was vulnerable.

Saint had altered her life as much as she had changed his. While Hunter missed those long, wild nights of debauchery with his friend, there was no doubt that Saint and Catherine were happy.

"It is so good to see you," she said, returning to his side. She surprised both of them by kissing him on the cheek. For a former brothel madam, Catherine did not like to be touched, and it was this elusiveness that caused the patrons of the Golden Pearl to claim her as their own.

Although he would never admit it to Saint, Hunter would have welcomed Madame V into his bed if she had deigned to return his flirtation. Frost, on the other hand, had bedded the lady when Saint had abandoned all hope of claiming her affections. There had been a few weeks last summer when Hunter had wondered if Saint was going to throttle Frost over an incident that occurred years ago and had more to do with easing loneliness than with love. Still, if Frost was smart, he would refrain from mentioning the brief affair in Saint's presence.

Catherine smiled up at him. "We are fortunate to have such a good friend."

"Very nice," Saint drawled from the doorway. "I discover my dearest friend fondling my wife in my drawing room."

Unabashed, Catherine glanced back at her husband and grinned. "Really, love, being ravished in the drawing room sounds too civilized." She winked at Hunter and walked over to Saint, who automatically enfolded his lady in a possessive embrace. "You are well aware that I want to be adventurous now that you've turned me into a staid married lady."

If Saint had been genuinely jealous, Hunter would have offered an explanation and an apology. However, none was required. Saint knew his friend was honorable, even when caught in a compromising embrace with his wife.

Saint cupped Catherine's face and kissed her, infusing enough passion into the gesture that Hunter wondered if he should take a walk in the back gardens.

"No one could accuse you of being staid," his friend said, not taking his gaze off his wife's face. "And later, I will prove to you that being ravished in a drawing room can be exciting."

"Promise?" She playfully tugged on his cravat.

"You can trust me," he assured her. "When I am finished, you will be unable to enter this room without blushing."

"It is apparent you both are too distracted for a visit." Hunter retrieved his hat from a table and headed toward them. "I will call another day."

"Don't be an arse," Saint said, keeping his arm around Catherine's waist. "Sit down and tell us why you are here."

"Oh, that is simple enough," Hunter said. "My betrothed is in London, and she intends to marry another man. I need some advice on how to court the lady. Otherwise, I will likely put a bullet in the first gent who offers for her hand."

Chapter Twelve

"I'm so pleased you are amused," Hunter muttered crossly.

Saint had been laughing for a solid five minutes. The only thing preventing Hunter from punching the happy bastard was Catherine. While she had seen her fair share of violence over the years, it would be rude to pummel one of his dearest friends in the lady's drawing room.

"Forgive me, my friend," the marquess said, trying to catch his breath. "How many times did you manage to lose your lady?"

"I did not precisely lose her," Hunter protested. "She left with her servants, and I deigned not to follow. Lady Grace has the unfortunate habit of not staying in one place."

"How long have you been betrothed to this young woman?"

The question came from Catherine. Hunter gave her a sheepish look. "Since I was twelve."

Catherine's gray eyes widened in surprise as she

soundlessly counted the number of years that had passed. "Nineteen years is a long time to be betrothed. In all the years you patronized the Golden Pearl, you never once mentioned this marriage arrangement."

Her soft condemnation was stinging, even if it was well deserved.

"I mean no insult, dear lady, but our association was strictly business. You provided me with nightly amusements, and I made you a very rich woman," Hunter said bluntly.

A soft oath rumbled in Saint's throat; his fury at the reminder that his lady had once peddled flesh and sin to the wealthy was evident. Catherine laid her hand on his forearm. The tender gesture kept her husband from tearing Hunter apart, for which he was grateful. He had no desire to fight his friend.

"You are correct, of course," the marchioness said, her smile stiffer and less welcoming than it had been before.

Hunter instantly regretted his words. He had come for their help, not to upset either one of them about the past.

"Even if we had been friends, you likely would have never heard of Lady Grace Kearly." He sighed with resignation. "I rarely spoke of her, even to my closest friends. Saint will attest that I am speaking the truth."

"He is," Saint said, still sounding furious on his wife's behalf. "Regardless, he owes you an apology."

Before Hunter could open his mouth, Catherine was shaking her head. "I do not require one. Nor should you insist," she said, sensing her husband was planning to demand it regardless of her wishes. "He has been a good friend to both of us, and I trust him to keep our secrets."

"You humble me, my lady." Hunter would have preferred that she slapped him for his callous comment.

"I disagree," she countered. "You were there the night my husband confronted Mulcaster and Royles. You delivered the punishment they deserved for hurting one of my girls, and even managed to impress upon them that spreading rumors might shorten their miserable lives. In many ways I owe you."

Hunter's forehead furrowed. "How so?"

Catherine glanced at her husband. "You and Frost kept Saint safe, even when he was determined to do something foolish like challenge Mulcaster. To this day, the gentleman keeps his distance for fear of pricking the temper of any Lord of Vice."

"Royles never told him the truth about you," Saint said, his voice roughening as he struggled with his anger.

"I am well aware of it," she said, her gray eyes warming with amusement. "If he had, I suspect both men would have succumbed to untimely accidents."

"If Mulcaster ever figures out that he knew you as Madame Venna, I might have to do more than break his jaw," Saint said, meaning every word.

"And I can direct you to several locations where one can conceal a body." When he and Saint stared at her in grim astonishment, she added, "Why are you both surprised? Running a brothel is a dangerous business. It was one of the reasons why I decided to close the doors to the Golden Pearl."

It was time to change the subject.

"So tell me more about your Lady Grace."

"The duke was following us."

Grace and Rosemary never made it back to their residence. The park was closer, and her companion insisted on hearing every detail without other people underfoot.

"I am not so certain," Grace countered. "He had already purchased the bouquets. I have it on good authority that His Grace is quite familiar with all the flower stalls in town."

On the day of their accidental meeting, the duke had been nearby because he had intended to purchase flowers for someone. This afternoon, he had claimed he had appointments—appointments that required small tokens of his affection.

There was nothing anyone could say to convince her that the flowers he had placed into her arms had been intended for her.

Recognizing that pained expression on her mistress's face, Rosemary gentled her voice. "Darling, you were so young when the marriage arrangement was struck. The duke was still a boy. That grand-mother of his had a way about her. She frightened fully grown men, so it wouldn't have taken much to bend a twelve-year-old boy to her will."

"What are trying to say, Rosemary?"

The older woman hesitated, unwilling to add to Grace's pain. "As you know, no one asked for my opinion at the time, and I would have given your grandfather an earful if I thought he might listen. Time has proven that the dowager should have waited until you were older before she bound you to her grandson. Perhaps, the duke would have not been so resistant to the notion of marrying you if he had had a glimpse of the lady you have become."

Grace thought of the miniature Mr. Porter had presented to her years earlier as a birthday present. His Grace had been several years younger than she was currently when he had posed for the artist. Even then, she could see the man waiting to emerge from the boy. Her heart had memorized every line of his handsome face. The color of his eyes and hair. The enticing curve of his lips. How many years had she dreamed of him kissing her?

And when Hunter and I finally met, neither of us recognized the other.

As a child, she had fancied that they were soul mates. Though separated by the passing years, des-tined hearts would recognize each other. The ro-mantic poets composed frivolous drivel. When she returned to Frethwell Hall, she intended to burn those silly passionate books that had led to her downfall.

Dear heaven, it hurt more than she could have ever imagined.

"Do you remember the miniature Mr. Porter gave me?" Grace said, feigning a calmness she did not feel. "He had told me that the duke wished for me to have it."

It had been a tiny falsehood on Mr. Porter's part to ease a young girl's sorrow. She had lost everyone who had been important to her, and was beginning to doubt the duke's affections for her.

Although she loathed admitting it, nature and time had improved upon the real man she had built her dreams of family and home around.

"Indeed, I had forgotten about it," Rosemary said, speaking of the miniature. "I thought you had consigned the blasted thing to an empty drawer and had not gazed upon it in years."

Grace grimaced, annoyed that she had neatly trapped herself with the old lie. How could she explain to Rosemary that she had retrieved the miniature within hours of abandoning it? The duke's portrait was still one of her most treasured belongings. She had even brought it to London, all the while knowing that the journey was her first step in freeing herself from an arranged marriage.

She shrugged. "I did. Nevertheless, I have spent my entire life waiting patiently for this man to claim me. Is it so strange that my curiosity drove me to pull out the trinket from time to time and study the face of the gentleman who was picked to marry me?"

"What's this?" Rosemary asked, stepping closer. "I thought we had come to London so you didn't have to marry the scoundrel?"

"We did," Grace protested, worried that she was feeling conflicted now that she had met the man. "I am. The duke's reaction was unexpected. I thought he would be relieved when I cried off."

"Need I remind you that His Grace was probably chasing ladies in Covent Garden?" The older woman uttered a wordless oath. "Do you need further proof that Huntsley is a debauchee? For all you know, he has several mistresses and a dozen bastards clinging to their skirts."

Grace's heart clenched at the possibility. She had been foolish to believe that the duke would have been faithful to a lady he never wanted to claim.

"What do you propose that I do?" she demanded, choosing anger over tears. "Lady Netherley has agreed to help me find a husband. The Duke of Huntsley has already proven untrustworthy. With my uncle plotting to seize my inheritance, I cannot afford to make any mistakes."

"That's my girl," Rosemary said, pulling Grace close and hugging her. "Now that we have recovered from all of this excitement, I suggest we return to the house and get something warm in your belly. Once you feel better, we can discuss our next step."

"Yes," Grace said, allowing the woman to guide her

toward the coach. "You take such good care of me, Rosemary. I don't know what I would do without you."

The woman who was the closest thing Grace had to a mother said, "And God willing, you never will."

"Honestly, I know very little about Lady Grace," Hunter admitted, meeting the Marchioness of Saint-hill's gaze. "The fault is mine. Porter sent me reports, but I rarely read them."

It was enough for him to know that the girl was being fed, clothed, and educated properly.

"You have been receiving these unread reports for nineteen years."

When put that way, he wanted to order someone to soundly beat him for his casual dismissal of a girl who had no one but him.

"Yes."

Though there was no accusation in her tone, his expression darkened. "We were betrothed as children, Catherine. A vast number of years have passed since that day."

"Cease teasing Hunter, love," Saint said, settling down beside her on the sofa. The gent could not seem to keep his hands off his wife. "Can you not see that he feels guilty for his neglect?"

It was not precisely true, but to deny it would cast him in an unpleasant light. "I am taking responsibility for her."

Catherine clasped her hands together. "Have you

considered that Lady Grace may wish to find someone else who might be more suited to her delicate
temperament?"

"Lady Netherley has decided to play matchmaker.
However, Lady Grace will have to struggle with her
disappointment," Hunter said, almost relishing the
battle between them. "A bargain was struck, and it
will be kept."

"This has more to do with your cousin than the
lady," Saint reminded him needlessly.

*And I have no intention of allowing the miscreant
to win.*

Feeling defensive, he demanded, "What does it
matter? Lady Grace will be my duchess."

She believes I have failed her.

Hunter was unused to failing at anything. It was
just one more thing he could blame Lady Grace for.

Catherine unintentionally darkened Hunter's mood
by giving him something he had never desired.

Pity.

"You are worried about her," Catherine said. Her
astonishment was another mental lash.

Before he could reply, Saint asked, "What about
Porter? Will she turn to him with the expectation
that he will assist her in finding a way to break the
contract?"

Hunter tugged at his cravat. He felt as if the fabric
were strangling him. "It's possible. This afternoon, I
left a message with his assistant. He has orders to
contact me the moment he hears from Lady Grace."

The doors to the drawing room opened, and Saint-hill's butler entered the drawing room. "Forgive the intrusion, milord. The Marchioness of Netherley has arrived, and she insists on an audience immediately."

"We have no time for ceremony, my good man," Lady Netherley said from the other hall. "Sainthill would never turn me away when I've come to discuss Lords of Vice business."

Saint glanced at Hunter. He shrugged, having no idea what news Vane's mother was anxious to share. Since he had been planning to visit the elderly marchioness this afternoon, her unexpected visit was fortuitous.

"Allow her to enter," Saint said to his butler. All three of them stood to await the lady's arrival.

"It is high time," Lady Netherley muttered as she leaned heavily on her walking stick to enter the drawing room. "I am too old to be—Saint, my dear boy! It is good to see you." Saint inclined his head so she could kiss his cheek. "And Catherine . . . that color is so pretty on you. It brightens your eyes."

"Thank you, Lady Netherley," Catherine said demurely. "Please join us. We were about to ring for some tea."

Hunter could not help but he impressed. One would think she had spent most of her life sheltered in the countryside. Of all the lady's guises, this one perhaps suited her best. Everyone adored her and, more important, she and Saint were happy.

Lady Netherley seemed overcome with relief when

she noticed Hunter. "What providence! I called on your residence first, but no one could tell me when you might return."

Hunter took her hand, and guided her to the nearest chair. "You were looking for me?"

"Indeed I was, dear boy," the elderly marchioness said, beckoning him to sit beside her. "This is my fourth stop. When you were not at home, I had the coachman stop at Nox—"

"You went to the club?" Saint asked, shaking his head as he walked by him and Lady Netherley.

No ladies were allowed entry into Nox. Their steward, Berus, must have been distressed to see the marchioness on the other side of the door.

She nodded. "I also called on my son and Dare's residence. No one was receiving visitors this afternoon. You and Catherine were to be my last stop before I headed home."

"What was so important that you were searching London for me?" Hunter asked, concerned.

Lady Netherley pulled out a small handkerchief that she had tucked into her sleeve and dabbed at her face. "It's about Lady Grace."

"What's this?" he exclaimed, coming to his feet.

"Sit down, Hunter," Catherine said, her tone sharpening to force his compliance. "Lady Netherley, is it true that Lady Grace has asked you to find her a husband?"

The elderly marchioness ceased patting her face at the question. "Quite. She's a beautiful girl, and such impeccable manners. I have little doubt that I will be successful in finding her a respectable husband this season."

Hunter inhaled deeply, working to remain calm. Throttling the old woman would not endear him to anyone. He tried a different tactic. "You came to deliver a message from Lady Grace, I assume?"

"A message?" The cataracts in her eyes gave the marchioness a slightly unfocused gaze. "Oh, no, not from Lady Grace. I came to tell you and your friends that trouble is afoot, Hunter."

He closed his eyelids and pressed his fingers against the tender skin. "You are not the first to bring such news, my lady."

"And I shall not be the last. I've come to warn you that your cousin has arrived in town," Lady Netherley said, her gaze never leaving his face. "The rumors have reached his ears. He knows that your lady is dissatisfied with the arranged marriage, and hopes to cry off."

"And my cousin?"

Not that he did not already suspect the truth.

Lady Netherley exhaled. "He is prepared to support her cause."

"The devil he is!" Hunter exclaimed.

Chapter Thirteen

"Lady Grace!"

Grace ruthlessly quelled the excitement that rose within her at the sound of the Duke of Huntsley's voice. She glanced up and noticed he had increased his pace to catch up to her and her companions. Was he afraid that she would run off? It did not signify that she had managed to avoid the gentleman for three days.

How had he deduced her whereabouts? If he had showed up on her doorstep, he would not have been able to charm the information from Rosemary. It was then that she noticed the two ladies with her had not spoken a single word. They appeared to be enthralled with the bonnets on display in the front window of the milliner's shop.

Good grief—had the outing been a ruse to lure her and the duke together? Were her new friends, Regan and her cousin Miss Bramwell, attempting to play Cupid on her behalf?

"What have you done?" Grace murmured to Regan, since she was standing the closest.

"Like it or not, the man is your betrothed," Regan said, smiling as she raised her hand in greeting to the approaching gentleman.

"Not for long," Grace murmured back. "Lady Netherley will find me a suitable replacement."

"I understand why you are angry," Regan said quickly, the earnestness in her tone the only reason Grace was not heading in the opposite direction. "Men can be ars—flawed."

Lady Bramwell giggled at her friend's very un-lady-like description.

"Hunter was wrong when it came to his dealings with you. He usually doesn't botch matters this badly."

"If you say so," Grace replied, too polite to contradict the lady's assessment.

The duke was closing in on them, so Regan had little time to debate Grace's sincerity. "However, those days are over and done with. Give him a second chance to know you, Grace. Hunter may surprise you."

Even when the gentleman was in the wrong, he exuded confidence. The grin on his face never faltered as he slowed to a more leisurely stride and then stopped before the trio.

"Good afternoon, ladies."

He bowed. All three ladies curtsied.

"Hunter, what an amazing coincidence," Miss Bramwell said, earning a sharp quelling look from Regan.

"Astounding," Grace said, her gaze drinking in the sight of him. His proximity always managed to send her heart racing. She wondered if she would ever grow comfortable in his presence. Then she remembered that there would be no reason to do so if he failed to meet the terms of the marriage contract. "It is as if Fate had a hand in our meeting."

Fate being Regan.

The young marchioness possessed a romantic heart. She was in love with her husband, so naturally she thought everyone deserved love matches as well. She had not believed Grace when she had confessed that any affection for the duke would end in heartache. Regan loved Huntsley like a brother or a cousin. She saw his faults but could not accept that he was innately cruel. And the young marchioness might be correct in her assessment of the Duke of Huntsley's character, but she was wrong about his ability to love. The romantic sentiment was something Grace often appreciated in novels and poetry, but it was too much of a leap to believe the duke would ever hold any affection in his heart for her.

"What has lured you ladies from the drawing room this afternoon?" he inquired, his eyes twinkling in amusement.

Regan gave Grace an apologetic glance, while

Miss Bramwell blushed prettily at the duke's question. Her reaction was telling in itself. How many ladies in London were secretly pining for the Duke of Huntsley's interest?

"Since I am new to town, Lady Pashley thought I might appreciate the London shops," Grace explained when her companions did not immediately reply. "Many of the new fashions are unsuitable for the country, and the village shops do not offer much in variety."

Hunter's eyes narrowed at her blunt reminder that he had left her to rot in the country, but he offered no apologies. If he expected her to be a meek creature, then he was bound to be disappointed. She had been queen of Frethwell Hall, even as a child. The tutors and governesses hired by Mr. Porter had insisted that obedience was admirable in a young lady.

However, it was one of the lessons that never quite stuck.

"Well, you are in luck, then," he said genially, unaware of her thoughts. "Both Regan and Miss Bramwell have exquisite taste and are well versed in the London fashions. Though, Regan, I do believe your husband would be happier if you raised the cut of your bodice now that you are a married lady."

Regan laughed, reminding Grace that her companion shared a friendship with the duke she had been denied. "Dare has better sense than to tell me how to dress. It's a viewpoint you would be wise to imitate if you wish to marry."

Grace found her own cheeks warming at the bold comment.

"Regan!"

"Forgive me," Regan said, slipping her hand through Grace's arm in a friendly manner. "However, I did tell you gentlemen have certain failings, and it is our responsibility to set them on the right course."

Hunter raised his eyebrows. "Then how do you explain your brother?"

"I don't," Regan said dismissively. "I'll leave that impossible task to another lady."

Miss Bramwell cleared her throat to get everyone's attention. "Since we are here, I would not mind trying on that bonnet with the pink satin ribbons. It would complement a dress I already possess."

"I second that notion," Grace said, seizing on the opportunity to send the duke on his way. "Besides, we have taken enough of His Grace's time. I am certain you have appointments."

"Not at all," the Duke of Huntsley said, his expression revealing he was aware that she was trying to get rid of him. "My afternoon is not encumbered with tasks, and it would be a rare treat for me to act as escort for three beautiful ladies."

He walked past Grace and opened the door. "Shall we?"

Miss Bramwell seemed as uncomfortable with the notion of Huntsley accompanying them on their errands as she was.

Regan walked through the door first. "Lovely. A pity we couldn't invite all the Lords of Vice," she drawled over her shoulder.

"Splendid," Grace said, surrendering to the undeniable fact she had finally gained the Duke of Huntsley's attention.

Chapter Fourteen

Hunter was having a grand time.

He doubted Lady Grace would concur. Perhaps he was being a tad unfair, intruding on her afternoon with Regan and Miss Bramwell. Without his assistance, she was making friends on her own. While he was pleased his friends had welcomed his reluctant bride-to-be into their small social circle, he wondered whom they would side with if the lady pressed her case to end their marriage arrangement.

Not that Lady Grace did not have good reason to be vexed with him.

He had not understood how badly he had muddled his affairs until she had caught him in what appeared to be a compromising position with Lady Cliffton. Damn Portia and his poor timing. He could guess the lady's intentions even if he had done everything to prevent her from spitting it out. The lady was unhappy with her marriage, and Hunter had once held a *tendre* for her. It wasn't arrogant to reason that the lady hoped to conduct an affair with him. He was certain that Portia had heard the rumors about him. His choice in lovers varied in hair color, size, and carnal appetites. Nevertheless, all of them had one thing in common—he preferred the unattainable. Whores and widows only craved his coin, while the occasional married lovers were more interested in gaining petty revenge against their husbands by taking a younger, more virile lover.

Although Portia's marriage had not been forged with the fires of passion, he had believed her to be strong in character and her reputation beyond reproach. She would have never considered having an affair with him years ago.

What had changed?

Hunter glanced in Lady Grace's direction. She had disappeared behind a curtain to be measured by the seamstress. Would his duchess feel the same way in the coming years when the title and wealth began to seem like burdens rather than privileges?

No. As cross as she was with him, he could see that she possessed a sweet disposition. She was patient with Lady Netherley and kind to his friends; she treated her servants as if they were family. She was not marrying him out of ambition or greed, but rather because a promise had been made when they were children.

And by everything he held sacred, the lady was going to keep it!

Miss Bramwell laughed at something her cousin whispered in her ear. Regan noticed his regard and gave him a saucy smile. The minx. Dare had his hands full with that woman. He also owed her an expensive trinket for sending him a note, telling him of her outing with Lady Grace.

A few errands, Regan's note had explained. His three female companions enjoyed quite a busy afternoon. They worked their way down several streets, visiting milliners, a draper, a bookseller, a hosier, a perfumer, and a fur and feather manufactory. He could not fathom where these ladies found the energy to peruse the inventory of every store.

Mentally, he was exhausted. He might have begged for their mercy hours ago, but he had something to prove to Lady Grace.

The lady belonged to him.

Straightening from his casual stance against one of the ornate posts that separated parts of the small showroom, Hunter made his way across the room to the closed curtain that separated him and Lady Grace.

Regan noticed his movements and rushed to stop him.

"What do you think you're doing?" she demanded, crossing her arms. "You cannot go in there."

He could have ignored her and pushed her aside. Not only was she Dare's wife, she was also the young girl he had had a small hand in raising.

Which explained why she was an opinionated, mischievous brat with no respect for her elders.

"You were the one who invited me," he reminded her. "What did you expect?"

Hunter walked around Regan.

"I didn't expect you to behave like an ars—"

He glanced back and noted that Miss Bramwell had clapped her hand over her cousin's mouth before she could finish her insult. It appeared he owed the lady a small gift as well.

Very few people got away with silencing Regan.

With a smirk on his lips, he walked the remaining distance to the curtain and slipped inside.

Lady Grace was alone. She whirled around, and a strangled gasp was wrung from her throat. "What are you doing? You cannot be in here!"

The lady's outrage barely registered. Hunter's mind went blank as he took in the state of her undress. The seamstress had removed her walking dress so measurements could be taken. Lady Grace wore only her stays, chemise, and petticoat. As he had already deduced, she was beautifully formed with long slender limbs and pale, soft skin unblemished by the sun.

She was currently using her lovely arms to hide the soft swells of her breasts. "Get out!"

Hunter sighed, enjoying her feminine outrage. He rather doubted she would be comforted by the notion that he had seen countless women with less clothing covering their bodies than her. "Forgive me, Lady Grace. I am reluctant to be a gentleman about this."

"Why the devil not?"

"If I leave, you will only find another reason to

avoid me. This way, you and I can talk and get to know each other." There was a simply constructed chair in the corner of the small private room. He grabbed the wooden frame and dragged it closer to her. Once he was satisfied with the position, he sat down. The wooden joints squeaked in protest but the chair held his weight.

Lady Grace frantically glanced around the interior. Espying her discarded dress, she scooped it up and held the bundle of fabric in front of her. "What if I call for help?"

"I would not recommend it," he cautioned, watching her struggle with the dress as she attempted to cover herself from his hungry gaze.

Hunter almost told her that it was too late. He had glimpsed enough, and his appetite was whetted. If she were already his lover, he would have pushed her against the wall, unfastened his trousers, and taken her swiftly. He would have kissed her, drinking in her cries of ecstasy to muffle the sounds of his rough pleasuring.

The lady standing before him would have been mortified and beet red all the way down to her toes.

She lifted one haughty eyebrow. "Give me one good reason why I should not scream?"

"Well, for one thing . . . every one in this respectable establishment will come running to see the cause of your upset. Then they will see me." He dug his right thumb into his chest. "Before nightfall, the *ton* will be abuzz with Lady Grace Kearly's scandalous behavior. I can hear the gossips just licking their lips. Lady Grace fornicating with a Lord of Vice in a dressmaker's shop? How shocking!"

Lady Grace worried her lower lip as she contemplated his words.

He and his friends had established their notorious reputation long ago. There was little that would surprise certain members of the *ton* when it came to the Lords of Vice. Including her in his tale added to the excitement.

And if I become any more stimulated, even an innocent like Lady Grace is bound to notice my cock poking the front of my trousers.

"All the more reason to leave."

Lost in his pleasant thoughts, he did not immediately follow her reasoning. "I beg your pardon?"

Lady Grace wet her lips. If they were dry, he would have been more than willing to moisten them with his tongue. In warning, his cock twitched and he resisted the urge to adjust himself.

"You have to slip out before you are discovered," she said in hushed tones and looked pointedly at the closed curtain.

"And miss our little chat? I think not," he said, grinning up at her. "If you had arrived in town earlier, we might have posted banns. However, all is not lost. I will apply for a special license. We can marry before your birthday and satisfy the terms of the contract."

Anger got the best of her, and Lady Grace stepped

toward him. "How many times do I have to say it? You had your chance to marry me, Your Grace. Now I have decided that I am no longer interested in adhering to the terms of this arranged marriage. I may need a husband before my birthday, but I will find another suitable man."

"Why do you need a husband before your birthday?" he abruptly asked, homing in on the odd comment. "If you allow the terms of the agreement to expire, you are a free woman, are you not?"

"What business is it of yours?" she heatedly countered, taking another step closer. "I will no longer be your concern. If I am a free woman, then I will handle my problems in my own way."

It took him seconds to figure out why Lady Grace was so eager to jump into another marriage so quickly. "It's your uncle."

"Leave my uncle out of this."

He clasped his hands together and rested his chin on them as he contemplated her outrage. "Of course. That explains much. You are an heiress, and a titled one at that. If you won't marry me, then I cannot fathom why you would be so eager to marry and bed some inferior gent if there was not another threat looming on the horizon."

"Some inferior gent?" She sneered at him. He should not find her fury so arousing, but he liked her spirited nature even if it would be the cause of many battles in the future. "Is your arrogance boundless?"

"Not in the slightest." Hunter startled her by

standing up. The light wooden chair toppled over. She tried to back away, but her overconfidence had brought her too close. He knocked the bundle that made up her dress out of her hands, and shackled her wrists with his fingers, using her desire to escape him to back her up until she was against the wall.

Just as he had imagined them together moments ago.

"Please . . . let me go."

Her green eyes were dark and filled with muted defiance. Good. He did not want her to fear him—at least not so much that his touch repulsed her.

"You have spent too much time in the company of servants, Lady Grace." She gasped as he abruptly raised her arms above her head and pinned them in place. "You will discover that a husband is not as biddable."

"You have no desire to marry."

"Think not?" He pressed his body against her. His cock thickened, straining to find the apex of her thighs and the yielding, wet sheath that it concealed. "My body's response proves that I am quite capable of performing my husbandly duties if you challenge me further."

Her eyes widened at his threat. "You risk a scandal on both our heads."

"My dear innocent lady, I was taking part in scandal after scandal while you were still learning to write your letters. You will discover that the gentleman you are about to marry fears nothing."

Her vulnerable position did not prevent her from fighting back. "Are you mad or simply too thick-headed to understand? I do not wish to marry you."

"Sometimes, Duchess, we do not have a choice in what we want in life," he murmured, his gaze lingering on her full lips. For once, the words were not spoken with the bitterness of a man trapped by his circumstances.

"You speak of duty," she said in a flat mutinous tone.

His thumbs brushed the tender flesh of her wrists. Her pulse was thundering in her veins as he slowly rubbed against her. "Aye. For years, I thought only of myself and the decisions made for me by my grandmother. I never considered your feelings."

"Would things have been different if you had?"

He felt the need to answer her truthfully. "No. I was a selfish boy who grew into a selfish man. A failing, to be certain, but I am willing to mend my ways."

Lady Grace blinked rapidly as if she were fighting tears. "Do not bother on my account. I no longer need you."

And she thought to replace him with another. Well, that would not do at all.

"That is where you are wrong, Duchess."

Her face was inches from his, but she managed to tilt her chin up and glare at him. "I am not your duchess."

"That, too, is where you are wrong."

Hunter had not intended to take his teasing this far, but Lady Grace was so damn defiant. He had to show her that the decision was out of her hands.

"Have you ever been kissed?"

"Of course I have."

Her answer gave him pause. Some country lad had been kissing his lady? He gritted his teeth as his grip tightened on her wrists. "Who?"

"Ah." Understanding lit her green eyes. "You do not like the idea of someone else kissing me, when I know that you have likely kissed thousands of women."

Aye, it was hypocritical of him to demand names of her bold suitors from her when he was guilty of the same deed. Not to mention all the other wicked things he had done. Still, fury roiled in his gut that other men had kissed her.

Instead of pressing for names, he tried another tactic. "Did you like it when these gents kissed you?"

"And what if I did?"

By God, the woman liked to prick his temper.

A man's patience only went so far. If she had not fallen so neatly into his verbal trap, he would have been tempted to toss her over his knee and paddle her backside for her audacity.

Fortunately for her, he had other, more pleasurable ways of expressing his frustration. "Then I intend to make you forget all the gents who stole a kiss from you, while you left them hoping for more than a chaste peck."

It was in her expression to respond to his assertion that the kisses she had received thus far had all been as exciting as kissing a relative, but at the last minute she thought better of it.

Good.

The lady was learning something about him, and he had yet to begin the lesson.

Instead, she said, "You can try."

Oh, it was rare for Hunter to refuse a challenge. He lowered his head and closed the inches between them. "And I will succeed, Duchess."

He captured her mouth before she could turn her face away. Her eyes closed as their lips connected. His tongue flicked lightly at her upper lip as he tasted her. Lady Grace's mouth was sweet for a lady who possessed a tart tongue. His mouth glided over hers, mentally willing her to give him more.

Innocence.

It was a flavor he had never cared to sample.

"Open your mouth, Grace. Taste me," he commanded while his hands massaged her wrists.

He longed to touch her, but he dared not release her. If given the chance, Lady Grace would likely slap him for his uncivilized behavior. And he would deserve it. Getting fondled by a man in a dressmaker's shop was out of most noblewomen's experience.

She managed to surprise him by parting her lips slightly. Or perhaps she was attempting to curse at him for taking liberties she had not granted him. None of it mattered, Hunter thought, as he pushed her further. His tongue glided against hers and he groaned against her mouth.

Christ! His cock was as hard as an iron spike in his trousers. Hunter pressed the length of it against her, craving nothing more than to raise her petticoat and sheathe himself fully. He was not considering the risks or the small matter of the lady's virginity.

This was all about need.

He needed to bury himself into this woman and stake his claim.

Hunter was almost mindless with it. He rolled his hips against her, imagining the feel of her tight, muscular walls as they squeezed his thick cock. The mere thought had him struggling not to release his seed.

He no longer had to deny himself.

Another demand his grandmother had imposed on him with her damn marriage contract was the expectation that he was to get his new duchess with child as soon as they were married.

In his current state, Hunter was rather looking forward to the task. In fact, perhaps if they were quiet, no one would realize . . .

"Good heavens, what are you doing to that young woman?"

Lady Grace froze and her eyes snapped open in mute shock.

The outrage in the seamstress's voice was nearly as effective as a bucket of lake water in winter. Hunter gave Lady Grace's slack mouth a final kiss before he lowered his head to gaze over his shoulder.

His body shielded his future bride from curious gazes; nor was he in any rush to display his full-blown arousal to a room filled with spectators.

Such a display had *scandal* written all over it.

While he could weather it with a smug grin on his face, he suspected Lady Grace would perish from the humiliation.

Or at least, she would want to.

"What do you think I'm doing?" he growled, hoping his anger would send the woman scurrying.

"You have no business being in here," the seamstress said.

Hunter silently cursed. Every female he encountered this afternoon was determined to be difficult.

"I said as much when you entered the room," Lady Grace muttered.

"Hush," he told her, and then softened the command by kissing her cheek. To the outraged seamstress, he said, "What do you think I'm doing, woman? I'm tending to my wife."

"I am not your wife," Lady Grace whispered back.

"Yet," he murmured for her ears only.

She tugged, and belatedly Hunter realized he had not released her arms. He unshackled her wrists and swiftly bent down to retrieve the discarded dress. He did not offer Lady Grace the garment. Instead, he held the fabric in front of his trousers. Even being caught in a compromising position had not lessened his arousal.

"Well, Your Lordship, that sort of tending best

be done in your bedchamber," the seamstress said sharply. "We run a decent place. We'll tolerate none of that tomfoolery here."

Hunter heard soft laughter. Regan. She would never let him live this down, but he hoped she would be kind to Lady Grace. He glanced in her direction; the rosy hue had not faded from her cheeks.

"I think—I—" He cleared his throat. "I will wait outside while you finish with my *wife*."

He emphasized their marriage status to spare Lady Grace further humiliation, just in case the seamstress thought to rebuke her once they were alone.

Thankfully, this reluctant bride did not contradict him.

"It is best that you do," the woman said, taking the wrinkled dress from Hunter. She glanced pointedly at the front of his trousers, and for the first time he felt a burning heat of embarrassment in his face. "Distance from your lady might ease your affliction."

Unable to think of a proper rebuttal, Hunter took the woman's advice and left the private room.

Chapter Fifteen

"I heard your meeting with Lady Grace went well," Saint said as they strode into Nox the following evening.

On most nights, Hunter felt a thrum of satisfaction at what he and the other Lords of Vice had created. While his grandmother might not approve of what he had done with the property on King Street, Nox had become a lucrative source of revenue. This evening, however, he surveyed the filled tables without much enthusiasm. He had spent a restless night plotting his next step with his future duchess.

"Was that sarcasm, Saint?" Hunter raised his hand to acknowledge several gentlemen who had called out his name. "I thought marriage had cured you of your jaded views toward the quest of love."

Saint smiled, enjoying Hunter's discomfort entirely too much. "So now you are in love?"

"Don't be daft, you arse," Hunter snapped back. "I just met the chit. Besides, love was never written into the marriage contract. My grandmother was a practical lady. There was no value to be gained by insisting that I love Lady Grace. As long as I marry her, increase the family's holdings, and produce an heir, I have satisfied the terms of the arrangement."

"It sounds cold."

"No, it sounds like the dowager," Hunter countered, annoyed that he had to offer an explanation. "Don't tell me that you have forgotten how she was. Or has Catherine addled your brains and turned you into a romantic fool?"

"I am in love with her," Saint freely admitted, looking far too happy for Hunter's querulous disposition. "As for a fool, I cannot say. Though if I had let her run off as she had planned, I would have lived out my life regretting it."

Hunter opened his mouth to say something spiteful, but thought better of it. No, he did not begrudge his friend's happiness. Had he not quietly observed Saint over the years as his friend's love for the woman he thought he could not have ate away at his soul? The marquess had been slowly withdrawing from the world, even his friends, and all of them would have done anything to save him.

Although it had taken him years, Saint had eventually summoned the courage to fight for the woman he had loved almost at first sight.

While his circumstances were not similar, Hunter had also allowed the years to distance himself from Lady Grace. There was no love lost between him and his bride. He was not even certain he liked her.

Still, he would honor his commitments, and the lady would, as well, even if he had to prod her with a pistol to gain her obedience.

"That look on your face always means trouble," Saint observed.

"What?" Hunter asked, confused before he realized that he had not offered his friend a proper reply to his question. "Forgive me, this business with Lady Grace has presented complications that I had not anticipated."

"Obviously."

Hunter ignored his friend's dry retort. "The lady is not what I expected."

"Sin told me that you deserve our pity. He said that your lady is a toothless hag who hasn't taken a bath in ten years, who possesses the booming voice of a giant—"

Hunter stopped and gave his friend an incredulous look. He threw his head back and laughed until his stomach ached. Several patrons glanced in his direction. It was unusual for him to lose his composure, but he couldn't help it. He had once thought uncharitable things about the lady.

"If Sin truly met Lady Grace, then he offered no such description to you," he said, attempting to catch his breath. "The Duke and Duchess of Strangham were purported to be an incredibly striking couple, and their daughter has been blessed with beauty."

Saint made a noise that indicated he was unconvinced.

"I have been her harshest critic, and I humbly admit that my assessment was based wholly on ignorance. Saint, she has a face that most women would envy. Delicate features, unblemished skin, and eyes the color of unripe olives. Her hair is thick, glossy, and the lightest of browns with a hint of gold woven within the strands of hair. She is petite, her limbs are finely formed, and her disposition is—"

"Akin to a harpy, according to Frost," Saint added.

The need to defend the lady rose within Hunter's chest—which, he was certain, was Frost's intention. "Frost dislikes women who are opinionated. Since he cannot seduce her, I doubt he lingered in her presence longer than a few minutes. Though I agree, Lady Grace does have her faults. She is outspoken, stubborn, and determined to thwart my attempts to honor this arranged marriage."

"She sounds like a scorned woman."

Hunter nodded. "With good reason. It didn't help that she caught me with Portia."

Saint's eyes widened in amazement. "Portia? Christ, what are you doing dallying with Cliffton's wife? I thought you ended your association with the lady years ago."

"Of course I severed all ties," Hunter said, frowning as he recalled how his old love felt in his arms. "I had already hurt her. Why would I compound the problem by ruining her marriage to Cliffton? No, the lady sought me out." And Lady Grace's arrival had prevented Portia from explaining why she had longed to see him.

"I shouldn't have to offer this advice, but I suggest that you stay away from Lady Cliffton. Lady Grace is skittish, and most women react badly when they encounter their husband's former loves."

Ladies were not the only ones who became a trifle upset about former lovers. There were several occasions when Hunter and his friends had to keep Saint from throttling one of Catherine's lovers. While the brief affair had meant nothing to her, Saint had not taken the news very well.

To Saint, he said, "What I shared with Portia is no longer important and none of Lady Grace's concern, so I would appreciate it if no one mentions Lady Cliffton's name to her."

Of course, his bride was brazen enough to bring up the lady on her own.

"So you do intend to marry her," Saint said, sounding pleased with the revelation.

"I have little choice," Hunter confessed. "I refuse to surrender my inheritance to my cousin, and the lady needs a keeper."

It might as well be him.

Espying the steward of Nox, Hunter and Saint switched directions and headed his way.

"Good evening, Berus," Hunter said, echoing his friend's greeting. "Any problems we should be aware of?"

"Nothing out of the ordinary," the servant said, signaling for brandy to be brought to the two men. "Though both of you might be interested in knowing that we had an unexpected guest three hours ago."

"Who?" Saint asked, taking a glass of brandy from the silver salver presented to him.

"Lord Mulcaster," Berus said, the name capturing both men's attention. "He played faro for an hour . . . lost . . . and then departed."

"Did he request to see anyone or talk to anyone?" Hunter asked.

"No, Your Grace."

"He must be getting desperate if he showed up here of all places," Saint murmured.

Hunter could feel satisfaction and eagerness radiating from his friend. "This isn't the first time Mulcaster has patronized Nox."

"No," Saint conceded. "However, his fortune has changed in this town. A part of him is beginning to wonder if it's mere coincidence or something orchestrated."

When it came to people hurting his wife, Saint was capable of ruthlessness. Mulcaster had made an enemy when he had befriended Catherine's foe.

"If that will be all, milord . . . Your Grace." Berus bowed respectfully. "I shall continue with my duties."

"The next time Mulcaster returns to Nox, I want to know about it. Send a messenger if necessary," Saint said.

"Of course, milord. I will see to the task myself."

Berus departed, tireless in his pursuit to ensure that Nox lived up to the high standards set forth by his employers.

Hunter turned to Saint. "What has changed?"

"Nothing. Everything is going as planned," his friend said, sipping his brandy nonchalantly.

"And what are those plans?" he asked, wondering if he truly wanted to know. Rumor had it that Catherine's despicable cousin, Robert Royles, had disappeared months ago, and Hunter wondered often if his friend had anything to do with it.

A man in love would go to great lengths to protect those he loved. Saint's next words proved it.

"Quite simply—I'm going to ruin the bastard."

A few days ago, Grace might have declared her evening a triumph.

She had attended three balls, had danced on seven occasions, and was savoring her new friend, Lady Pashley. Regan. Apparently, the young marchioness considered herself an expert on the Lords of Vice, and was quite sympathetic about Grace's predicament with the Duke of Huntsley.

As Frost's sister, she had been practically raised by the wild rakes. Many members of the *ton* thought this arrangement was imprudent, and would put the poor girl on a direct course for ruination. Her fascination with the man everyone called Dare only seemed to confirm it. When her brother caught her kissing his friend, he sent her away to a boarding school.

Isolated from the only family she had known, she had been miserable and lonely.

Regan's sentence had lasted five years.

So naturally, the young woman was appalled that the duke had left Grace alone for most of her life.

"Nineteen years," Regan murmured, shaking her head with disappointment. "If I had known, I would have traveled to Frethwell Hall each year."

The declaration warmed Grace's heart. "Thank you. I would have enjoyed having you there. Perhaps we could have conspired to lure the duke to come for a visit. Even so, I did have Mr. Porter. I always looked forward to his visits each spring. He was quite dedicated to his duties."

"Dedicated to Hunter, you mean," Regan said. Her esteem for the duke had plummeted when she learned how he had abandoned Grace to the country. "It also explains why Mr. Porter has neglected to contact you."

"I have come to the same conclusion," she admitted. "Now that the duke knows I am reluctant to go through with this marriage, he seems equally determined to see that I do. I find his change of heart bewildering."

"I do not," Regan said, opening her fan with a flourishing sweep of her hand. She gently fanned herself. "I believe I can offer some clarity to Hunter's disposition if you are interested."

"Of course."

"Direct your gaze to the right," she murmured,

using the fan to conceal her instructions. "Do you see the gentleman in the gold waistcoat?"

"Yes." To her astonishment, the gentleman was staring at her.

"The gentleman is Mr. Roland Walker."

The name was unfamiliar to Grace. "Who is he?"

"Hunter's cousin. A distant one. Neither man cares to acknowledge the blood connection. However, if you and Hunter do not marry, Mr. Walker will benefit rather generously from the discord."

Mr. Porter had told her that a portion of the duke's inheritance was in peril if the marriage did not take place. If he had mentioned the man's name, she could not recall. "This is the man who will claim the dowager's inheritance?"

"Precisely."

Then this gentleman would be on her side when she pressed her case. "I want you to introduce us."

Regan nodded, expecting this request. "I do not believe it will be a problem. He has been slowly making his way to you since you entered the ballroom."

Chapter Sixteen

"Lady Grace is dancing with my cousin."

Hunter stared at Vane in disbelief. "And you didn't stop them? What is the point of having you watch over her if you are going to allow a blackguard like Walker to approach her?"

The earl took a step back to give Hunter room to stand, but he was in no mood to defer to his friend. In fact, one might assume that Vane was angry at him.

"You asked me to discreetly observe her. I did," Vane said tersely. "She joined the ladies and together they have moved from ballroom to ballroom. Except for the dance invitations Lady Grace has accepted, she has rarely left Regan's side."

Lady Grace had been dancing with other gentlemen? Didn't these men know she was betrothed to him? "I want names."

"Of her dance partners? You can forget it," the earl replied, not understanding how close Hunter was to losing his temper. "I'll not be responsible for you putting a bullet into every gent who deigned to speak with your lady."

His lady. A detail Lady Grace Kearley was determined to ignore.

"How long has she been chatting with my cousin?"

Vane shrugged. "Long enough, I suppose. He did ask her to dance."

Hunter picked up his glass of brandy and finished it in one hearty swallow. "Has it escaped your notice that you left her alone with him?"

The accusation made the earl frown. "You told me to report anything unusual. Walker seemed to qualify."

Hunter slammed down the empty glass on the table. "I expected you to send a messenger and then put an end to Walker's mischief."

Vane snorted. "Oh, and having me, who is basically a stranger, drag Lady Grace away wouldn't have her screaming for a constable. And then I would have to explain to sweet and loving Isabel that I wasn't ravishing the chit, but rescuing her from your cousin who had only asked her to dance. No, thank you, I think I'll pass on that bit of lunacy."

When his friend described it in that manner, it did sound a little cracked. "That chit is ripe for the picking, and I wouldn't put it past my cousin to wonder if my inheritance isn't the only thing of mine he can claim."

"That's up to you." Vane raised his hands in surrender. "I'm done. If you're worried about Lady Grace, then it's up to you to protect her."

"The lady isn't too fond of me," Hunter grumbled.

"So change her mind." The earl gave him an exasperated look. "You can be charming. I've witnessed it on countless occasions. Tell me, how many women have you tumbled onto their backs with simply a grin and a few sweet words?"

His friend made it sound so simple. "Flattery will not impress this woman," he said flatly. He had injured her feelings, and she wanted his head on a platter. "This will require work."

Vane lightly slapped him on the cheek to get his attention. "The ones who matter always do, my friend."

"Why is Chillingsworth glaring at me?"

Grace tipped her head to the side to see what Mr. Walker was fussing about. The man wasn't exaggerating. Frost's expression had a tinge of murderous intent. From this distance, it was difficult to tell if the coldness in his regard was personal or a false impression perpetuated by the chandeliers blazing overhead.

"Have you recently offended Lord Chillingsworth?"

"I avoid the gentleman. He has a certain reputation with his fists."

"I suppose he's a respectable shot as well."

"So I have been told," he said, dismissing the earl

with a careless shrug. "Do you know him? Perhaps he views you as his?"

Mr. Walker managed a guileless expression, but Grace wasn't fooled. "Come now, sir. Can you not think of one more reason why the earl might be troubled that you are speaking with me?"

"You know who I am, don't you?"

"I paid attention when Lady Pashley introduced us," she said kindly. "More important, you neglected to explain your connection to the Duke of Huntsley."

His sheepish smile was endearing, but it did not soften her heart. "Ah, you have caught me. How embarrassing!"

For some reason, the males in the duke's family believed she was gullible; it was reason enough for her to walk away. What prevented her from leaving was Frost's hostile reaction. It made her curious. Was he spying on Huntsley's behalf? If so, the man would live to regret it. Huntsley, too, if she had anything to say about it.

"Yes, it is," she said mildly. "Is there a reason for this ruse?"

"Forgive me, Lady Grace. I was not certain you would speak to me," he replied.

His apology seemed sincere. Still, she was not convinced that he did not have other reasons for not mentioning that Huntsley was his cousin. "No one has mentioned you by name. I was aware, however, that the duke's grandmother added a clause in the marriage contract to ensure her grandson's compliance. If this marriage does not take place, you will be a rich man, Mr. Walker."

"I am not a poor man, Lady Grace," Mr. Walker protested.

"No, but men are peculiar animals. I would wager that rich gentlemen dream of growing richer," she said, softening the accusation with a smile.

Mr. Walker's expression lightened, and he returned her smile. "Yes, my lady, there are no limitations when it comes to wealth. There is another reason why I want Huntsley's inheritance."

"What reason is that?"

"I would enjoy claiming it because it was his. It would infuriate him to lose his grandmother's gift to me." Noting the puzzlement in her expression, he added, "Boyhood rivalry, I must confess. Huntsley and I never played well together. Both of us ended up sporting bruised eyes whenever the families came together."

"So where do I fit into all of this, Mr. Walker?"

He stepped forward. From the corner of her eye, Grace noticed that Frost had moved closer, too.

"Ah, I would be honored if you addressed me as Roland. We are almost family, after all."

"Almost, but not quite, sir," she corrected flirtatiously.

"Would it be impolite of me to speak of rumors that I have overhead about you and the duke?" he politely inquired.

"What did you hear?"

"That you might be unwed on your twenty-first birthday."

"I would not be the first lady to celebrate thusly."

"Do not be coy, my lady," he countered, unable to contain the excitement on his face. "You speak boldly, and it is one of the reasons why you fascinate me."

Grace doubted the duke shared Mr. Walker's opinion.

"You approached me because you wish to know if these rumors are true."

"And clever, too." He took up her hand, and kissed her lightly on her gloved knuckles. "Another admirable quality."

"Let me guess. Perhaps one you would like to explore further if the Duke of Huntsley is no longer barring your path?"

"It's a reasonable aspiration," he said, still holding her hand. "So tell me, dear lady . . . dare I stand a chance to earn your affections?"

"Well—"

"Take your hands off my wife, Walker!" Huntsley ordered, his menacing approach causing the couple to separate.

The duke's claim ignited her temper. "Your arrogance is astounding. I am *not* your wife, nor will I be if you persist this way."

This was not going well.

Hunter had managed to silence everyone in the ballroom with his declaration, giving everyone a chance to hear Lady Grace's biting response. If he had the ability to blush, he would as red as his hostess's headdress.

Walker had released Lady Grace's hand, but he was emboldened by her rejection of Hunter's claim. Circling around Hunter, he said, "I beg you, cousin . . . persist."

"It is so typical of you, cousin," Hunter sneered. "Hiding behind a woman's skirt. If you have something to say, at least have the pluck to say it to me instead of skulking around ballrooms in the hope of cornering my betrothed."

He had used *betrothed* in deference to Grace. If she denied him again in front of the *ton,* she would not be pleased with the results. Thankfully, the woman had the sense to hold her tongue.

"Cousin, no one could accuse me of skulking. Our hostess welcomed me with an affectionate embrace, and I am acquainted with several of the guests. When I learned your lady was in attendance this evening, I felt duty-bound to seek out an introduction. After all, she will be family." Walker deliberately shifted his gaze to the clearly vexed Grace. "Or not."

Any other day, Hunter would have called Walker a liar. This would have prompted an unpleasant confrontation, which would have forced them to excuse themselves. Once they had found a private setting, he and his cousin would have proceeded to pound out their mutual frustrations upon each other.

It would have meant leaving Lady Grace.

In her current mood, the violent confrontation with his cousin would only prove that he was unworthy of her. If she disappeared, he might not discover her whereabouts until her birthday had passed, and Walker would win.

He couldn't allow either one to happen.

Instead he swallowed his pride and bowed. "Forgive my tardiness, my lady. If you are agreeable, would you join me so I can make a proper apology in private?"

A few of the guests around them chuckled. No man wanted to humble himself in front of witnesses, even when he deserved it.

Hunter offered her his arm, his level gaze silently willing her to take it. He was not above carrying her out of the ballroom over his shoulder, but he was trying to prove to her that he could be polite.

Lady Grace glanced from one man to the other. She was too astute not to realize that the cousins could come to blows if Hunter remained. "Of course, Your Grace," she said meekly, and placed her hand on his arm.

Hunter wasn't deceived by her obedience.

"Mr. Walker, I am so pleased we were able to meet," she said genially.

His cousin inclined his head. "I look forward to our next encounter."

"It will be soon, cousin," Hunter said silkily. "I pray you will be able to join us as we celebrate our wedding day."

"Of course," Walker said tightly. "The joyous nuptials have been long in coming."

"If ever," Lady Grace said low enough that Hunter was the only one who heard her.

As Hunter and his future duchess strolled across the ballroom, he realized this was the first time they were appearing together as a couple. He nodded to familiar faces, and Lady Grace smiled shyly though he did not halt to make introductions. Hunter's gaze connected briefly with Frost's. His friend shook his head as if he was disappointed in him. It was his friend's not-so-subtle way of telling him that he should have punched Walker and have been done with it.

Hunter relished the notion of seeing his cousin with a split lip and broken nose, but that was selfish. He had Lady Grace's sensibilities to consider. Ladies tended to be squeamish of men who bloodied their fists and then wanted to put their hands on their women.

Though it surprised him, the desire to put his hands on Lady Grace was stronger than his need to bruise his knuckles on his cousin's face.

They did not speak until they had left the crowded ballroom. He directed her to the left and down several stone steps until they reached a small alcove cut into the hedges.

"Would you have truly fought him?" Lady Grace asked.

"It is likely," he confessed, assuming that she

would prefer the truth. "Walker and I have never gotten along."

"Which is why your grandmother chose to give your inheritance to him," she shrewdly concluded.

"Aye."

His dislike of Walker was a powerful incentive for him to honor his word.

"Did you order Frost to watch over me?" she abruptly asked.

"Uh, no," he replied, deciding not to mention that Vane had been the one watching her. Perhaps Vane had warned Frost of Walker's presence before he had left the house to find Hunter. "If Frost was following you, he must have noticed that Walker had entered the ballroom. Our mutual dislike is hardly a secret, and my friend was probably concerned that Walker would approach you."

And Frost was correct. As usual.

"You were not tardy."

Hunter feigned innocence. "I beg your pardon?"

"You were not planning to attend the ball. Regan would have told me," she said, convinced she had secured the lady's loyalty.

She probably had.

Regan loved the Lords of Vice as dearly as she loved her brother, Frost. Nevertheless, as with most siblings, the two often experienced differences of opinion. Once Regan had heard of his indifference toward the lady he was supposed to marry, she had sided with Grace. Dare's wife knew exactly how Hunter had been spending his time over the years, when he should have been courting his future duchess.

Perhaps Regan was not the best choice in friends for Grace.

When he pulled her aside, he would have to remind the lady that some stories about the Lords of Vice should not be retold. Not everyone was as forgiving as she was.

Hunter gestured for her to sit on the marble bench. "I lied to Walker, though you are clever enough to guess the why of it." He sat down next to her.

Lady Grace did not try to move away from him. "I assume you were worried that I would tell him about my decision. You need not have worried. Mr. Walker has already heard the rumors."

Damn.

"Did he mention who was spreading these rumors?"

She shook her head. The paper lanterns in the trees overhead revealed her elegant profile. "No, he did not mention who had told him. However, he was cheered by the news and decided to seek an introduction."

Walker had come to London to gloat over his victory. "His intention was to make certain that you did not alter your decision."

Lady Grace frowned. "But I have not."

"You have," Hunter said, his tone daring her to argue. "There is more than just my inheritance at stake, Grace. Have you ever wondered why your grandfather was willing to betroth his only grand-daughter at such a young age?"

Grace contemplated his question. "He had recently lost his wife, daughter, and son-in-law and was grieving. Perhaps he worried that he did not have long to live, so he appealed to your grandmother for assistance. It was a respectable match for her only grandson, so she proposed a merger between the two families."

"A plausible explanation, but there was more to this arrangement than increasing my family's wealth as you suggested the other evening," he said, carefully choosing his words. "In most cases, your father's heir . . . his brother would have been declared your guardian."

Forgetting that she disliked him, Grace turned toward him. "Rosemary told me that my uncle refused to be burdened with a child," she explained.

"Who is Rosemary?"

She grimaced at his bewilderment. "You met her the other night, and the afternoon at Covent Garden. The day we were betrothed, Rosemary was there in the library. She was my nurse. As I grew older, she stayed and became the housekeeper of Frethwell Hall."

Her affection for the woman was reflected in her expression and voice. For her, Rosemary was more than a servant. She had become her friend, adviser, and companion.

And Rosemary wanted him out of Grace's life.

That much was clear when he saw the woman's face after she opened the door.

"What I know of your uncle and grandfather are written on the pages of my grandmother's journal, and the letters she had exchanged with your grandfather. I know there was some concern about your uncle. He had been with your father when he had had his accident, and while a formal inquiry exonerated him, your grandfather was worried that your uncle might have had a hand in your father's death."

"Rubbish," she protested. "My uncle is not an affectionate man—"

Hunter silenced her with a gesture. "Your uncle has visited Frethwell Hall?" He closed his eyes and answered his own question. "Of course he has called on you."

He had not realized the extent of his failings until her admission. Porter only visited once a year, and the servants would have yielded to the Duke of Strangham's request to visit his young niece.

"How often did he visit?"

She must have realized that she had given away a secret. "Not often," she hastily confessed. "He never visited when my grandfather lived. A few years after his death, my uncle called on me to pay his condolences for my loss. He was kind, and I was—I needed kindness."

Grace was a vulnerable girl and the bastard ruthlessly took advantage of her grief.

"Rosemary remained at my side the entire visit," she added, sensing his fury that he had not anticipated—and worse, had not cared—how the girl was faring after her grandfather's death. "A few years passed before we saw him again. He never stayed long. My uncle was just concerned. He had learned in London that you opposed the match, and were doing your best to forget my existence."

She bowed her head, her expression a mix of sadness and shame.

Hunter wanted to flog himself for his selfishness.

"It wasn't you," he whispered. Although he had not earned the right, he reached out and traced the curve of her neck with his fingers. "I was young, wild . . . arrogant. I thought only of my own needs. It was wrong, and I would not blame you for despising me."

Her head lifted in astonishment. "I do not hate you, Your Grace."

"Hunter."

Defeated, she sighed. "Hunter. We were both too young to offer much resistance to our family's wishes. I am old enough to understand the reason why you preferred to forget about me, and a part of me even forgives you."

It was an olive branch he had not expected.

"You do? Then we can—"

"Which is why I cannot marry you," she said, speaking over his suggestion that they marry immediately.

Hunter tensed. "Why are you being so stubborn about this?"

"Because I think we both deserve a chance to be happy." Grace stood before he could stop her. "I deserve to be happy."

"By marrying a man handpicked by Lady Netherley?" he thundered, enraged at the thought.

"I might." She grinned down at him. "Is it any different from marrying you?"

"Christ . . . damn it," he swore, rising to his feet and stalking after her. "Yes, it is. I am the man your grandfather entrusted to marry his granddaughter."

"He was wrong."

It was a painful admission, even if it was the truth. "I have disappointed you, and there is nothing I can do to alter the past. However, I can change the present and our future. Your uncle—"

"Cannot be trusted any more than you can be," she finished for him. "No, I refuse to listen to your promises of a rosy future."

Hunter grabbed her by the arm and pulled her against him. "Who promised you a rosy marriage, Lady Grace?" he asked roughly. "You have already deduced that I am not a good man."

"No . . . you are dangerous," she whispered, her head tipping back as he pulled her closer.

"Our marriage will not be something to feather the pillow of a young maiden's dreams. It will be tumultuous because you like to defy me. You may spend your days doing as wish, but your nights belong to me." He caressed her face. "I am a demanding lover. Each night I will strip you naked and explore every inch of your body. My tongue will taste the unique flavors of your curves, as I pleasure you with my hands . . . my coc—"

"Enough!" she begged.

Her body trembled against his.

"You will beg me, Duchess. However, it won't be pleasing for me to stop. Once I have claimed your body, you will hunger for my touch."

"Never!"

"Such a little innocent. I have had years to hone my skills, Grace. You will not resist me for long. Why deny yourself? I will employ everything I have learned to pleasure you. Soon your body will long for me. It is only a matter of time that your heart and mind will follow. I will instruct you—"

"Please." She closed her eyes as if the gesture could silence him.

"Yes, to please me," he said, allowing himself the luxury of rubbing his aroused body against her hip. "I promise you that you will relish everything I will do to you. So much so, you will want to explore me as well. I look forward to the night you ask to take my c—"

She placed her fingers over his mouth.

He nibbled her gloved fingers, parted them with his tongue. "Into my mouth, Grace. Over and over. Night after night. You will take me as a lover and rejoice in our joining."

She cried out a soft denial, but Hunter was in no mood to soothe her. Perhaps he had frightened her a little with his needs, but she had had nineteen years to prepare for him.

He suddenly realized he was tired of waiting for her.

Hunter nudged aside her fingers and captured her mouth. He was not gentle in his claiming. His mouth slid over hers, rubbing and teasing until she parted her lips. It was an invitation he could not resist. He pushed his tongue, demanding entry, and she was too innocent to deny him. She stiffened when his tongue stroked hers, but she did not make the mistake of biting him. At first, she merely endured. He could only imagine her maidenly thoughts as his mouth hinted at the carnal demands of his body.

If there were no fear of discovery, he might have laid her down onto the grass. He could have pleasured her and himself without removing their clothing. All he had to do was unfasten his trousers and—

"Enough," he rasped, tearing his mouth away from hers. His hand slid to his swollen cock, which was pinched at an unpleasant angle. To free himself would only end with him taking her innocence here and now.

"Go. Return to the ballroom," he said, breathing heavily as he battled his desire to take her. "Regan will keep you company until I return."

"W—what about you?" Grace stammered, sounding winded.

"I need a few minutes." How did one explain the workings of man's body to an innocent such as his duchess? "Just leave me."

She mistook his harshness for rejection. "Fine! But don't bother searching for me. I will be leaving immediately. In a matter of days, I will no longer be your concern."

"Grace, wait," he called out, but she was already stomping away in a high fury. Nothing he could say would convince her that he had sent her away for her own good.

"Great," he muttered, reaching for the buttons of his trousers before his lust twisted his damn cock off.

Chapter Seventeen

"I'm pretty certain kidnapping is considered a crime."

Hunter wondered if Regan would forgive him if he quietly strangled her husband. His defense, should it be required, would be that the gent had provoked him.

"Really?" he drawled. "Tell me again the romantic tale of how you convinced Regan to marry you without her brother in attendance?"

Dare, the annoying hypocrite, had climbed into his lady's window and proceeded to seduce her. Once he had gained her cooperation, he had whisked her off to be secretly married before Frost had deduced his friend's plans.

Hunter marveled at Frost's restraint for not murdering his new brother-in-law when he learned of the couple's elopement. There was no doubt that the two men occasionally disagreed about what was best for Regan. Nonetheless, Regan was in love with her husband, and the one person Frost genuinely loved was his sister. He would never do anything to ruin her happiness.

"I did not kidnap Regan." Dare frowned. "Not precisely."

"What my husband is trying to say is that I was a willing participant, once I was aware of his plans," Regan said, carrying several blankets for their journey.

Behind her, Frost and several servants followed, their arms laden with provisions that they would need for the journey.

"'Tis a pity no one felt inclined to share these plans with me. I might have offered to give you a proper wedding," Frost said coolly.

He might have accepted Regan's marriage to Dare, but he was not above reminding them that they had excluded him from the festivities.

Regan crossed over to her older sibling and kissed him on the cheek before he could turn away. "I had a proper wedding, as you call it. What would have made it perfect was having you beside us."

"Do I need to remind you that you forbade me to speak to your sister?" Dare asked, sounding annoyed.

Frost dismissed the old troubles between them with a wave. "I'd rather not. The rehashing of old news will turn an already trying journey into days of misery. I, for one, am in favor of forgetting the whole thing."

"Thank you, brother." She hugged her brother, then slipped her unencumbered arms around Dare so she could embrace both men. "I'll admit I have a few trepidations about leaving our son behind while we go on an adventure."

"He won't even notice you are gone," Frost argued, earning a sharp pinch on his arm. "Ow . . . damn harpy!"

"I am his mother. Show some respect," she grumbled, her face darkening with worry.

Hunter felt a stab of guilt. Perhaps he had been selfish to ask Dare and Regan to join them on this trip to Gretna Green. The couple had seemed the right choice because Grace and Regan had become close friends over a short period of time. They were similar in age, and both ladies had grown up without a mother to guide them. He had thought Grace would be amendable to being kidnapped if she was surrounded by friends.

"If you must decline, I will understand," Hunter said, wondering if he could convince Saint and Catherine to join them.

"Nonsense," Frost said, speaking over his sister. "The boy will be fine without his mother and father for a few days. Juliana will spoil him as if he were her own babe, and Sin will protect all of them with his life."

Regan's lower lip trembled as her eyes filled with unexpected tears. "I know." She sniffed. "I will just miss him."

Dare gathered his wife up into his arms and embraced her. In her ear, he whispered, "Come away and misbehave, and we might be able to give our spoiled boy a sibling."

Regan laughed. "Oh, you would like that, would you not?"

"Yes." Dare's gaze shifted to his friends. "That is, if we can find a moment or two to slip away from our chaperones."

Hunter and Frost walked to the other side of the coach as Dare continued to tease and whisper wicked promises into his wife's ear. Her laughter filled the air.

"Dare has a way with Regan," Frost said, staring blindly down the street.

"He loves her, Frost."

His friend grunted, accepting the explanation, even if he had never experienced the feelings himself. "It's a good thing Dare can charm his way out of trouble. When Regan figures out that you intend to marry Grace with or without her permission, you will lose her support."

"Then we will refrain from sharing that detail of the plan with her," Hunter said, telling himself that this was the wisest course. The elopement would solve most of his problems. Grace's uncle would no longer be able to challenge Hunter's rights to her inheritance, and his marriage would put an end to his cousin's hope that he might one day claim the dukedom.

Once he was married to Grace, getting her with child would quell any remaining arguments.

All he needed was for Grace to agree.

Although she denied it, the picnic along the river had to be Regan's suggestion. The demands on Hunter were numerous, and Grace could not believe he had decided to shirk his duty to spend the afternoon with her.

"He's courting you," Regan had confided. "Give him a chance to prove to you and himself that you mean more to him than keeping his word to his grandmother."

Clearly, her friend saw something in him that others had not. She did not trust his sudden concern about her welfare, and her uncle had managed to plant his own seeds of doubt about the duke's motives for marrying her. Her uncle insisted it was greed. He reminded her that her inheritance had been claimed by Hunter almost from the beginning. He had nurtured and broadened her investments, and thanks to him she was a very rich woman. Her uncle explained that over time Hunter had come to view these investments as his own.

Hunter's cousin, Roland Walker, had his own theory about Hunter's affection. He claimed his cousin was driven by pride. Mr. Walker argued that not only did the duke covet her wealth, but he was also determined to fulfill the conditions of the marriage contract set forth by his grandmother. Otherwise, he would have to forfeit certain properties that were owned by the dowager and were not connected to the dukedom. If Hunter failed to marry Grace before her birthday, then Mr. Walker would inherit the dowager's lands.

Grace had witnessed the rivalry between the two cousins. Hunter was adamant that he not lose his grandmother's lands to a cousin who did not deserve them.

Was the inconvenience of an arranged marriage just another sacrifice allowing Hunter to keep what he thought as his? Both her uncle and Mr. Walker had presented a valid case for her to distrust Hunter.

If not for Regan promising that her husband and Frost would be joining them on the picnic, Grace might have refused the invitation.

They had left town to find a tranquil spot along the river, and the two-hour journey north had been worth it. The landscape was breathtaking and in its own way reminded her of Frethwell Hall. She had forgotten how much she missed the quiet beauty of the countryside. It was almost as if they were the only people left in the world.

"More wine?" Hunter asked solicitously.

With Regan, Dare, and Frost as chaperones, the duke had not tried to kiss her, which was a pity. The wine had warmed her belly and spread to her head. If Hunter had invited her to stroll along the banks of the river, she would have accepted. Away from their friends' watchful gazes, he would have kissed her.

"I shouldn't really," she said, wrinkling her nose. "You've poured two glasses into me."

Hunter filled her glass anyway. "It is a picnic. You are supposed to overindulge."

Grace nodded, and pleased him and her by taking another sip. "I do not have a problem with gluttony. It's making a fool of myself in front of you and your friends that worries me. I am unused to this wine."

She scowled when Hunter's face blurred. "I do not feel . . . something." Grace shook her head and was grateful when the duke's handsome face came into focus. "There you are. I feel strange."

Hunter reached out to prevent her from losing her footing. "Finish your wine, and then you can take a nap if you wish."

Grace tipped her head back in an exaggerated manner and swallowed the final drops. She laughed, unable to prevent the glass from slipping from her fingers.

"So clumsy." She attempted to reach for the glass but Hunter caught her hand and pulled her close.

"Don't worry about it. I have plenty more," he assured her as the world spun them around.

The edges of her vision darkened. "Hunter?" she gasped, fear lacing her voice. "I am losing you." Again his face blurred.

"No, my stubborn girl, I've got you," he said, picking her up and cradling her against his chest.

In the distance, Grace heard Regan cry out. She turned her head but the movement made her dizzy. A single word echoed in her fuzzy head.

Wrong . . . wrong . . . wrong.

She tried to speak, but the sounds coming from her lips made little sense to her.

"Grace, let go," he commanded.

How does he know I'm falling? she mused before succumbing to the darkness waiting to claim her.

"You drugged her?" Regan shouted at Hunter as he carried the now unconscious Grace to the coach. "How could you!"

"I had no choice," he muttered, glancing back to see that Dare and Frost had already packed away most of their possessions while he had kept a watchful eye on Grace.

Instead of falling asleep, Grace had proven stubborn even when under the influence of wine laced with laudanum. She had gotten up and walked to the river's edge. The goal, as Frost had pointed out, was not to drown her into compliance.

By then, Regan was beginning to suspect their afternoon plans had been altered.

"Grace trusted you, you arse," Regan said, pounding her fists against his back while he struggled not to drop his sleeping bride.

"Dare, a little help," Hunter called out. If his friend got her hands on something heavy, she was likely to bring it crashing down on his head. "Regan, I'm doing this to protect her."

"You are doing this to protect yourself." She raised her fist again, but Dare grabbed her wrist.

"Enough," her husband said as Regan struggled to

free her wrist. "You've given him enough bruises. And it's safe to say that he deserves them all."

"I do," Hunter assured her. "You may not approve of my method, but time is running out. Everyone has an opinion, and many of them are not in my favor."

Regan made a scoffing sound. "Do you expect me to pity you?"

"No." Hunter gritted his teeth. He was unused to explaining himself, but he needed Regan's assistance if he ever hoped to sway Grace. "I understand that you are vexed with me—"

"*Vexed* barely covers what I feel right now."

He nodded, belatedly realizing that he had to earn back Regan's trust as well as Grace's. "I deserve every insult, and when I have more time, I will allow you to verbally flail me for tricking Grace into traveling with us to Gretna Green."

"You shouldn't worry about me. Think about Grace."

"I am thinking about Grace," he shouted back. "And me, as well. Regan, the lady was surrounded by foes. Her servant Rosemary has been whispering vile things about me for years. She had convinced Grace that I had abandoned her."

"You did," Dare and Regan said in unison.

"That is hardly the point," Hunter growled, settling into the seat with his precious burden. "Rosemary had already convinced Grace that she should break the terms of the contract, and then find a husband in London."

"From where I'm sitting, it's a sound notion," Regan said, climbing into the compartment of the coach and sitting on the opposite side so she could spend the long journey glaring at him. "I am even willing to help her if she orders you to turn the coach around."

Frost poked his head through the doorway. "Regan, you are being too hard on Hunter. While I may not exactly agree with his methods—"

"You were the one who suggested the laudanum in her wine," Hunter fiercely protested. Sacrificing his friend gave his sister's wrath another target.

"Frost!"

He did not bother appearing contrite. Regan was too angry to notice anyway. "The laudanum was supposed to make her tired. She would have fallen asleep and we would have headed north." He nodded in Hunter's direction. "She would have awakened, and figured out that this was her wedding party. It would have been up to him to convince her to marry him."

"Get into the coach, Frost," Dare said behind him. "Hunter, we're ready to leave."

Regan's face softened as she stared at Grace. The lady truly cared about her friend, and suddenly Hunter felt like a brute for frightening her.

"How long will she sleep?"

"Hours . . . half a day. It depends on her." He brushed a strand of hair from Grace's face. "She told me that she hasn't been sleeping well. She misses Frethwell Hall, and there have been other concerns."

Like me.

Regan smiled, and it wasn't friendly. "Good. Then you have hours to convince me about why I shouldn't drug *your* wine and abandon you at the first inn."

Hunter silently appealed to Dare and Frost for help, but he had created his own mess. "Let's start with why Grace's grandfather approached my grandmother."

"I've heard the story," she said, yawning.

"Parts of it," he agreed. "However, not everyone knows the whole story. I didn't even know until I took a closer look at my grandmother's old papers."

"Very well. Tell me what you found." She pinned him with a look. "But don't expect me to forgive you for a very long time."

Regan was offering him an olive branch, and Hunter seized it with both hands.

Chapter Eighteen

Grace awoke to the sound of laughter.

She opened her eyes and was astonished to find herself in a bed. Sitting up, she grabbed her head and moaned. Then she recalled the wine Hunter had poured into her glass. How many glasses had she imbibed? Two, three . . . four?

It would certainly explain why her head was pounding and her throat was parched. She winced as the door opened and Regan appeared in the doorway with a tray laden with food and a pot of tea.

"The innkeeper needs to oil the hinges," Grace said, pressing her finger to her forehead.

Regan grimaced in sympathy. "Forgive me for waking you. I thought you were overdue for some food."

"I am," she croaked, and then grinned. "I guess my throat needs oil, too."

"How are you feeling?" Regan placed the tray on the mattress. "Be honest."

"As if I've been licking the plaster from the wall."

Grace stretched her arms, noting the various aches in her limbs and back. "I also feel rested. Did I humiliate myself by drinking too much wine?"

Regan hesitated. "Not precisely. What do you recall?"

"Nothing important." She frowned. "The picnic. Laughing at your brother's stories, and drinking wine. Feeling dizzy. Was I sick?"

"Hunter mixed laudanum into your wine," her friend said bluntly.

For a few minutes, she did not speak. Finally, she asked, "Why would he do such a thing? Was he trying to poison me?"

"Of course not," Regan said, preparing a cup of tea for her. "The laudanum was Frost's idea, but I'm not certain you should blame him. More and more, I suspect our nurse dropped him on his head when he was an infant."

Grace allowed herself to be briefly distracted by the notion of Frost as a child. He must have terrified the servants. "What about Hunter? Should I blame him?"

"Oh, most definitely," Regan said lightly. "Though to be fair, I can promise he has suffered for his sins while you slept."

"Good." She nodded approvingly. "You are a wonderful friend."

Regan glanced away. "I would have been a better one if I had deduced what the gents had planned when they proposed the picnic."

"What was their plan?"

She handed Grace her tea. "Nothing too outrageous. The plan was to kidnap you, stuff you in a coach with some amiable companions, and journey to Gretna Green before your uncle figured out Hunter intended to marry you."

"No," Grace said without thinking. "I will not agree."

"Regan forgot to tell you the best part," Hunter said from the doorway. "The part where I have days to wear you down and you finally agree."

"Never!"

Hunter made a soft tsking noise. "Never is a long time when one is sitting on a mattress dressed only in her chemise."

Grace seized the hard roll from the tray and flung it at his head. She missed. "Beast! Fortune hunter! Seducer of innocents—get out!"

He bent down, picked up the roll, and placed it on the table. "Only one applies, love. During the journey north, you can decide which one fits."

"Get out!" Grace reached for the teapot.

Regan shook her head. "I warned you."

"Make certain she eats something," Hunter said to Regan before he closed the door.

Grace fought back tears. She was confused, and more than a little frightened. At some point she had fallen asleep, and now she was ensnared in a nightmare.

"He's not a fortune hunter," Regan murmured.

"His father and grandfather squandered the family's fortune and then had the good sense to die. Hunter was raised by his grandmother. I have no doubt she was a shrewd old woman, and she made a point of teaching him everything that she knew. He doesn't need your inheritance, Grace."

She wiped away her tears. "That's not what he told me."

"Whatever he told you was a lie."

"Tossed you out of the room, eh?" Dare observed when Hunter had rejoined him and Frost.

"Not exactly," he coolly replied. "I retreated when she reached for the teapot."

His friends winced as they nodded in sympathy.

"I never considered that Grace might hold a grudge," he said, struggling not to feel sorry for himself. "Regan promised to help me sway Grace, but I don't think she is having much luck."

Frost chuckled and took a sip of his ale. "And you trust Regan to keep her word?"

"She's your sister!" Hunter protested.

"Not to mention, my wife." Dare glared at his brother-in-law. "You will show her some respect, or I won't stop her if she feels a strong urge to break some crockery over your thick skull."

The last thing this ill-fated journey needed was more bad luck.

"No one will be breaking dishes." Hunter sounded unconvinced; females were so damn unpredictable.

"And Grace will marry me once we reach Gretna Green."

Frost snorted. "Care to wager on it, gent?"

Without hesitation, he said, "Yes."

"How much?" Dare asked, his eyes lighting with interest.

As two men debated over their friendly wager, Hunter thought about Grace sitting in the middle of the bed. She had been too angry to notice that her chemise revealed more of her body than it concealed.

He had been willing to undress his future bride, but Regan had insisted on taking care of her friend. When he tried to insist, she reminded him that he had plenty of obstacles to overcome when it came to Grace.

"Are you in?" Frost asked, referring to the wager.

Hunter nodded. Aye, he was committed. He was laying everything on the line and betting everything on Grace.

Never had he been so uncertain of anything in his life.

Grace was running out of time.

They were hours away from Gretna Green, and soon the duke would demand a reply to the same question he asked daily. On second thought, it was not exactly a question. Hunter had a way of turning everything he asked into an order.

"You will marry me."

For days, she had managed to avoid giving him

the response he longed to hear. Regan applauded her efforts. Her friend thought it was fitting that Hunter suffer for assuming he could trick her into traveling to Gretna Green by slipping laudanum into her wine.

What if Regan hadn't been along to dissuade the gentlemen? Would Hunter have kept her drugged until their arrival? Appalled by her accusation, he had taken the time to assure her on several occasions that he wanted to put some distance between her and London.

Poor Rosemary. She must be frantic with worry. Unfortunately, Hunter was less sympathetic now that he knew the older woman had pressed for Grace to seek a more respectable gentleman.

Hunter angrily told her that her uncle had little interest in Grace marrying anyone. He implied that if her uncle had his way, she would imbibe the juice of the poppy on a daily basis since it had transformed her into an agreeable person.

He had been angry at the time he had made his prediction, so she was not certain if he was teasing. It was her fault. Since the day she had awakened in an unfamiliar bed, Grace had rebuffed Hunter's attempts for reconciliation.

When he had calmly announced that she would be sharing a bed on their journey north, Grace had put her foot down and insisted that she and Regan would share the inn bed. Naturally, her husband had been disappointed by the decision, but he wisely remained silent.

All three gentlemen were aware that she had not forgiven any of them, so they were attempting to make amends in their own fashion. Frost tempted her appetite by procuring her sweets; Dare entertained them by sharing stories that involved various members of the Lords of Vice.

Initially, Hunter had been vehemently opposed to the idea. However, her laughter had forced him to reconsider. She assumed the tales that were shared were heavily edited so Grace would not judge them too harshly.

In particular, Hunter.

She often caught him staring at her with an odd expression that might have been fear, though she could not imagine him being afraid of anyone or anything. Neither could she envision him accepting his grandmother's dictates without a certain amount of resistance.

So while the dowager lived, the young man had quietly chafed against the restraints she had used to tether him. Later, when he had found himself alone, his resentment had shifted from his grandmother to Grace.

After all, she had been the only one who stood between Hunter and his freedom.

Now she was willing to grant him the reprieve his grandmother had always denied him, and he was furious that she had power over him.

She tried to tell him that she was not interested in playing games.

His cynically retorted that all women played games.

Throughout this battle of wills, Regan pleaded with Grace to give Hunter a chance. She still had not forgiven him for truly kidnapping her friend, but she had known the Lords of Vice for most of her life. They were many things, but they were not intentionally cruel.

So each night she waited for Hunter to ask the same question. Each night she turned him away. With the horses eating up the miles, Grace could feel the duke's weighty stare as Regan, Dare, and Frost dozed within the confines of the coach.

"It's time. No more games, Grace," Hunter said, keeping his voice low so as not to waken their companions. "I'll have your answer, and don't disappoint me."

"What is your question, Your Grace?"

She sensed more than saw his grimace. "Will you marry me?"

Grace hesitated. She was not trying to be difficult. Half of her life she had often longed for the day he would claim her. The other half, she had come to accept that he had abandoned her. Though he refused to see it, there was a third choice. She could celebrate her twenty-first birthday as an unmarried lady. If she was strong enough to hold her ground, she could free them.

With a sigh of wistful regret, she said, "No."

Without warning, Hunter pounded on the trapdoor to get the coachman's attention. "Stop the coach!" he ordered, his harsh command waking his sleeping companions.

Regan yawned and blinked. "Has something happened? Are you two fighting again?"

"No," she said.

"Yes," he said.

The coach slowed, finally coming to a complete stop.

"Hunter, what mischief are you planning?" Frost drawled sleepily.

"Correcting a misunderstanding," he said as he opened the door. He grabbed her by the hand and pulled her along as he disembarked from the coach. "To protect her tender feelings, I told Grace that she had a choice about marrying me. I wanted a willing bride in my bed, and I believed that she would make the right decision on her own."

"I have a choice," she insisted stubbornly.

"No, you don't." He placed his hands on her waist and effortlessly lifted her, shifting her from the coach's steps to the dirt road. "And neither do I. It's time for both of us to stop behaving as if we do."

Chapter Nineteen

Two hours later, Grace married the Duke of Huntsley.

Five hours into the marriage, she was quite willing to have it annulled.

Grace gasped as her husband entered the bedchamber and shut the door. "Get out!" she hissed, seizing the sheet from Regan's hands and using it to cover herself. "You have no right to intrude upon my bath."

"I have every right, *wife*."

Approaching the two women with a nonchalance that only inflamed her outrage and embarrassment, Hunter sat down on the wooden chest at the end of the bed. He crossed his arms, his gaze meeting hers. She sank deeper into the tub.

Having known Hunter for most of her life, Regan was the only one who was not intimidated by his presence. She stepped in front of Grace, effectively blocking his view of his naked bride.

"Really, Hunter," she said in a chiding tone. "I would expect this high-handed conduct from Frost and possibly Sin, but this is beneath you."

Grace tilted her head to peek around Regan's body and glimpsed a quick flash of white as Hunter smiled at her. "Since you and your husband assisted me in kidnapping my reluctant bride, your lofty perch seems rather wobbly, my dear."

"Oh for goodness' sake!" she exclaimed, her arms rising along with her voice and exasperation. "If you had shared the details of your plan, I would have refused to have any part of it. The only reason why I stayed was the fact that no one could talk you out of it, and someone had to be on Grace's side."

"A warning that this madman was making plans to lure me away to Gretna Green would have spared all of us a long trip," Grace muttered under her breath.

Regan glanced back, her expression full of sympathy and guilt. "You could not run from him forever, Grace."

Hunter chuckled. "If she had tried, she would have found herself trussed up like a bird for the oven."

Regan's head snapped in his direction. "You are not being helpful," she said before she offered him her back. To Grace, she said, "Ignore his brutish manner. Even if he will not admit it, his intentions are honorable."

"A few more days and the contract would have been broken," she argued stubbornly. "I was almost free."

Of him.

She did not speak the words but they pealed like a

church bell in the ensuing silence. Regan grimaced as Hunter climbed to his feet.

"Unfortunately for you, my duchess, you have been soundly caught," Hunter said, glaring at her as he moved closer to Regan. "You bear my name and my ring on your finger. There is only one more task to undertake before we leave this village."

"Hunter."

He placed his hands on Regan's upper arms and began to guide her to the door. "Be grateful that we do not need witnesses for this part." Hunter glared at the frightened maid hovering near the tub. "You there. Your services are no longer required. Out you go."

"Aye, Your Grace." The servant dipped into a hasty curtsy before she rushed to the door as if her skirt were on fire. She was gone before Hunter could escort Regan to the door.

"This is not the way to go about this," Regan hissed at him as she struggled to free herself from his unyielding grasp. "Can you not see that the poor girl is terrified?"

Hunter and Regan glanced in Grace's direction. She tightened her hold on the sheet wrapped around her wet body and attempted to appear delicate and frightened. In truth, her heart was pounding with anger more than fear. He had thwarted all efforts to nullify their marriage contract, and now they were man and wife. The least he could do was leave her in peace while she sulked about her predicament.

Hunter switched his attention back to Regan. "You haven't been married long enough for me to consider you an expert on marriage. And let us not forget, your marriage was an unexpected event. I might have missed the fun, but I heard all the details on how Dare slipped into your bedchamber and carried you off to the nearest vicar."

Grace blinked in surprise. Dare had abducted his lady from her bed? Regan had mentioned that she had fallen in love with her husband when he still considered her a child rather than a young woman, but she had skipped some of the most fascinating parts of the tale.

"You most certainly did not hear *all* the details," Regan shouted at him, poking a finger into his chest. "Dare is a gentleman. He would never speak disrespectfully of me."

"Not with you in earshot anyway," he shot back at her. "He likes having you in his bed. The man isn't a complete fool."

"Neither are you," Regan countered. "So why are you behaving like an utter arse?"

Grace brought her fingers to her lips to conceal her smile. She would have never had the courage to deliver such a bold insult to Hunter. Even though Regan had played a role their elopement, Grace could not help but admire the young marchioness. She hoped to count her as a close friend one day.

Hunter frowned at Regan as he opened the door. "Your opinion is noted, Lady Pashley. Why don't you run off and share it with your husband and brother. There now, off you go." He gave her a not-so-gentle push.

"But—"

He closed the door, muffling the rest of Regan's protest. For good measure, he locked the door and pocketed the key. The marchioness gave the door a frustrated thump with her fist, but then fell silent. Unless she had rushed off to get her husband to break down the door, Grace suspected that she was on her own.

Hunter dusted off his hands, his expression revealing he was quite pleased that he had won that battle of wills. All of a sudden, his body stilled as if he just remembered that he was not alone.

He lifted his head until their gazes locked. He offered her a roguish smile. "Am I not a lucky gent? A naked wench in my bedchamber. It's my favorite way to while away an evening."

Regan had distracted him from more important matters, and that was how he should handle his new bride. Grace was crouched low with a damp sheet covering her and the bathtub like a tent. Her attempt at modesty was endearing, but his duchess was losing the battle. As the thick linen soaked up her cooling bathwater, it revealed more than it concealed. He thought about waiting her out because in another fifteen minutes or so, his view was going to become positively entertaining.

"I am not naked," Grace said rather waspishly as she adjusted her hold on the sheet covering her breasts. "Nor does this room belong to you. I have claimed it, so find another."

If she thought to distract him by drawing his gaze to her cleavage, it was working. Although he had not had the pleasure of viewing them without the hindrance of clothing, the generous swells hinted that he would not be disappointed.

"The room may not be mine to claim, but you, my delectable duchess, are." Hunter took an intimidating step closer, and she sank lower into the tub. "Do you require my assistance, or can you manage to get out of the tub on your own?"

She blushed. It was a reminder of her innocence and the sheltered life she had lived before he had married her. As a general rule, he had stayed away from virgins, who feathered their pillows with dreams of marrying a wealthy nobleman. His grandmother had bound him to Grace just as he was figuring out that girls had other talents besides being a nuisance. Dewy wide-eyed innocents were not for him, so he sought out the wicked and the reckless, earthy wenches who understood that his interest in them was fleeting. Along the way, there were one or two ladies who might have captured his heart if his grandmother had not sold it when neither he nor Grace was old enough to appreciate its loss.

"I will tend to myself once you leave the bedchamber," his bride said with steel threading her voice.

By faith, her courage was admirable. Unfortunately, it would take more than cheek to win this battle.

"A reasonable suggestion, Duchess," Hunter said, slowly circling the tub with his hands crossed behind his back. His actions forced an uncomfortable Grace to shift to protect her backside. "Though I respectably must point out a small flaw to your plan."

"And that is?"

He paused to admire her wary, albeit defiant expression. "I have no intention of leaving this room till morning."

Chapter Twenty

"B-but you must!" she sputtered.

Hunter leaned forward until his nose was inches from hers. "Contrary to your wishes, Duchess, what I must do is finish this business of making you my wife. A real marriage requires that I bind you to me legally and by flesh. I cannot sire my heir if you remain a virgin, now, can I?"

It was far cry from the honeyed words he was capable of uttering when he wanted a woman in his bed. However Grace had a manner of engaging him that was provoking as much as it was arousing.

"There is no reason to be coarse, Your Grace."

"My little innocent bride . . . you think honest speech is coarse?" Hunter reached out, and she flinched away. He lowered his hand. "If I had chosen to be coarse, I would have declared that I intended to fuck you, my lovely bride. How ironical that it was my blood that was spilled the afternoon the marriage pact was made, and now yours will be shed to signal its fulfillment."

His words and proximity threatened to break her composure. Grace blinked rapidly and glanced downward at her sodden sheet as if it were her shroud. "Of course, I understand that a woman is supposed to submit to her husband. However, I expected you to be . . . different."

Hunter scowled at her. What precisely was she accusing him of being? A sodomite? Or worse—impotent? "Different how?"

Grace shrugged without looking up at him. "You have managed to ignore my existence for the past nineteen years. When you insisted on going through with the marriage, I assumed that we would continue to live in separate residences."

Hunter stared down at her, silently willing her to meet his gaze. She must have exhausted what had seemed like an endless supply of impudence. He was quite surprised by the anger her assumptions about their marriage elicited. Granted, he had treated her shabbily, and might have continued to do so if not for the stipulation that he had to marry Grace before she turned one-and-twenty.

His grandmother knew him well.

He had not thought about his relationship with his duchess beyond marrying the chit and consummating the union. Since he had met Grace, he had given a lot of thought to the consummation part. His wife was extraordinarily beautiful. Bedding her was a task he intended to savor. If he had bothered to pay attention to Mr. Porter's reports, he might have sacrificed the few remaining years of his freedom and married her years ago.

It definitely would have spared him the hasty jaunt to Gretna Green.

"You were a child for the better part of those nineteen years," he said gruffly. "And I did not possess the inclination or the patience to have a girl underfoot."

He felt a stab of guilt when she gazed up at him with pain in her eyes. "You have made it abundantly clear that I am a nuisance, Your Grace. Forgive me, if my expectations for a proper marriage were dismal at best."

A proper marriage? Until recently, Hunter had not been intimately acquainted with what that entailed. Vane, Dare, Sin, and Reign claimed they were content to leave their bachelor days behind them, and their ladies seemed equally pleased with their husbands. There had been moments when watching the intimacy between the couples had been almost painful to observe. It had made him feel wistful, as if he had been missing something in his life.

Then he remembered the marriage contract.

And Grace.

The notion that she had been waiting for him should have eased his loneliness. Instead, the damnable contract had been a reminder that his grandmother's ambitions had managed to cheat him out of finding true happiness. A blissful joy that his married friends had found, while he was to be denied.

It had just been one more thing to resent Grace for.

"It is time to amend your expectations, Duchess," Hunter said, moving away from the tub while he removed his evening coat. He tossed the garment on the nearest chair, and his fingers went to work on the glass buttons of his waistcoat. "I have no desire to argue with you on the finer points of what makes a proper marriage, but one thing is certain—this is to be a true marriage. You will be my wife in all ways, and if you need guidance on your duties, I am acquainted with a few married ladies—"

"Just a few?" she mumbled under her breath.

Hunter's eyebrow arched in bemusement that she was brave enough to toss his past conquests at his feet like a gauntlet. She was going to need her bravado if she was going to get through their wedding night without tears. "I know enough. My expectations will not be too trying for you. First, we will be residing under the same roof, and you will welcome me into your bed regularly and—"

"Enthusiastically?" she added, not sounding too happy about the prospect.

He fought back a grin as he untied his cravat. "Don't fret, my dear. You will never have to feign your eagerness." The cloth landed on top of his discarded waistcoat.

Her eyes narrowed at his arrogant boast. "You think not?"

"No lady has ever complained," he replied flippantly just to see her eyes flare with indignation.

Grace did not disappoint him. Even with a wet sheet wrapped around her, she managed to look like a duchess sitting in a fashionable drawing room. "Should I ask for references?"

Hunter coughed, practically choking on his own spit. He could think of several former lovers who were outrageous enough to offer his new duchess their recommendations. "Quite unnecessary since I'm willing to prove myself." He braced his backside against the edge of the bed while he set to work on removing his boots. "And I have been more than patient. What shall it be, Duchess? Will you leave your cooling bathwater willingly, or shall I join you?"

She hesitated at the choices presented to her. Either way, he would have her. "The tub cannot accommodate both of us," she protested, staring at him warily as his second boot struck the floor.

Ah, she was such the little innocent. "It might be snug, but I believe we both will fit. I'm willing if you are."

"No!"

He halted at her emphatic command and gave her an expectant glance.

"If you leave the chamber, I will tend to myself."

Barefooted, he padded over to her. "If I leave you alone, you are bound to escape through the window."

"I most certainly would not," she said, insulted by the very suggestion that she was a coward. "We are married, and I have no intention of shirking my duties as the Duchess of Huntsley. I do, however, deserve a measure of privacy while I prepare myself for you."

Hunter was tempted to acquiesce to her request. His bride was no coward. Even so, anger kept the fear at bay, and he preferred to keep Grace's mind off what was to come. No, if he left her alone, she would only fret over matters that were beyond her control.

"No," he said flatly.

She seemed taken aback by his response. "No?" She gestured at the pile of towels on the chair along the wall. "Very well. I need something to cover myself."

Her command was not unexpected, but her maidenly modesty was not welcome in the bedchamber. Hunter had always insisted that his lovers be experienced to avoid the predictable complications of bedding a virgin. Grace was the exception to this specific rule, though he had no intention of offering her explanations.

"You might as well drop the sheet, Duchess. The only place you are going is my bed."

Grace rose unsteadily in the tub. No doubt her legs had grown numb folded beneath her like a hen on its nest. "Then I shall get the towels myself," she said imperiously, though she made no move to get out of the tub.

It was then that Hunter noted that his bride was trembling. He lost all patience with this particular battle of wills. "I've had enough of this." He marched over to the tub and swept her into his arms.

Grace gasped as the world tilted sideways. Without thinking, she slipped her arms around his neck to prevent herself from falling. "Put me down—"

A strangled scream escaped her lips as Hunter carried her to the bed. The soggy sheet that had been protecting her modesty fell away and landed onto the floor with a distinctive *plop*.

Grace surprised him by tightening her hold around his neck and burying her face into his shoulder. She mumbled something but her words were unintelligible to him. His poor little bride was probably affronted by her predicament. However, one way or the other, he would have stripped her of the sheet when they had reached the bed since he had no interest in sleeping with a bundle of wet linen between them.

"Don't fret about the sheet, Duchess," he said, lowering her onto the mattress. The servant had already turned down the bedding, which made his task simpler. "A dry bed . . . more comfortable than the tub, is it not?"

His furious bride rolled onto her side, muttering to herself while offering him a generous view of her unblemished back and buttocks as she tugged at the blankets to drag them over the lower half of her body. His grandmother had often told him that Grace would grow into a ravishing beauty. Good breeding, she had said, not that he cared at the time.

Now that Hunter had gone ahead and married her, he was appreciating his good fortune. He reached his hand out with the thought of caressing her back. He wondered if her pale flesh felt like silk.

Grace abruptly turned back to confront him, her eyes blazing with silent fury. "I may be your wife," she said crisply. "However, I deserve more respect and consideration than you carting me about the room like a wicker hamper!"

Hunter tossed his head back and laughed heartily. It was a perilous thing to do in front of an enraged female. More than once, he and his friends had gotten into various scrapes for their inappropriate sense of humor.

"Trust me, Duchess," he said, rubbing away the pain in his side. "Even foxed, I can tell the difference between a naked wench and a hamper."

Grace drew the blanket higher over her breasts. "I cannot tell you how much better I feel, knowing that I have such a clever husband," she said, managing to appear haughty even though she sat in the middle of the bed with only the bedding to protect her modesty.

Not that it was much of a shield. Hunter had gotten quite a good look at her body, and he was looking forward to doing more than just admiring her beauty. He wanted to spend the night caressing her skin with his fingers, learning the curves of her body. With his tongue, he would soon taste her most sensitive flesh and inhale the unique scent of her as he enticed her to arousal. And, finally, when he had claimed her innocence and showed her what awaited her beyond the discomfort, he would hear the soft sounds she made when she discovered the joys of the marriage bed.

It was time.

Tugging the final button on his shirt free, Hunter pulled the fabric over his head and tossed it with the rest of his attire.

"What are you doing?" she asked, her voice softening with sudden wariness.

"Nothing sinister, I assure you," he said, striding over to the nearest table and snuffed the candles. "Just preparing for bed."

Hunter left the candles near the tub burning as he returned to the bed. He assumed his shy wife might prefer the darkness, but he would not be doing her any favors by allowing her imagination to escalate her fears of him or their marriage bed.

He gave his chest a passing glance as he casually rubbed his flat stomach. Although he was not prone to vanity, his former lovers had often admired his body and his skills at bringing them pleasure. For some odd reason, he wanted Grace to find his physique praiseworthy as well. Possessing a reputation as an unselfish lover, he was prepared to demonstrate there were certain benefits gained from his rakish ways. He had every confidence that his wife would find their marriage bed quite satisfying.

Unfortunately, his duchess did not seem to appreciate her good fortune. Her face took on a chalky cast at his approach. She was unused to seeing so much bare male flesh, and he had not considered that his virility might overwhelm her. Perhaps it would have been prudent to leave his shirt on.

"Will you be dousing all the candles, Your Grace?" she asked in a weak voice.

"Hunter," he absently replied. "I think it is best that we keep the remaining ones lit. Are you not curious about your husband?"

Grace audibly swallowed.

"Here." He captured her hand and pressed her palm to his stomach. "You are free to explore me at your leisure."

In response to his invitation, Grace's eyes fluttered upward into her skull and her body slumped back against the pillows.

The little innocent had fainted.

Chapter Twenty-one

Grace felt a slight sting to her cheek. Bringing her hand to her right cheek, she opened her eyes and glared at the gentleman hovering over her.

"If you persist, I will have a nice bruise to complement the healthy color in my cheeks come morning," she said, attempting to sit up. When the duke refused to move, she simply pushed him away. "What happened?"

"You fainted," Hunter said grimly.

"Truly?" she said, sounding as surprised as she felt. She had knocked the wind out of her lungs a time or two when she was a child, but she could not recall a single incident when she had actually lost consciousness.

"Does this happen often?"

"I beg your pardon? Oh, the fainting, you mean." Grace shook her head. She adjusted the sheet covering her breasts, briefly wondering if her husband had peeked while she was indisposed. "No, I am not prone to the vapors. How long was I insensible?"

"Not very long," he replied, studying her face. "A minute, or so. How are you feeling?"

Grace pretended to ponder the question as she silently debated telling him the truth. If she lied and told him that she felt unwell, the deception would most likely allow her to hold on to her innocence for another day. It was the least her husband deserved for his high-handedness on this marriage business.

"Well . . ." She made the mistake of meeting his gaze. His eyes narrowed at her hesitation, and she sensed that the duke was expecting her not to tell the truth.

As if she was the kind of person who habitually uttered falsehoods to get her way!

Naturally, a little creative fibbing to get her way was one thing, but no one had ever accused her of being a coward or shirking her duty. The notion that he thought her capable of it was unbearable.

"It is kind of you to inquire, Your Grace. I am feeling quite better, thank you."

Her declaration did not appease him. "At supper, you barely ate enough to sustain a bird. Perhaps I should summon the innkeeper and have him prepare a tray."

"I am not hungry." Grace reclined back against the pillows, a willing sacrifice. "Forgive me for interrupting you. Pray continue."

She closed her eyes and awaited his ravishment.

What sounded like a cross between a groan and a

muffled laugh rumbled in Hunter's chest. Grace tried not to cringe as she felt the mattress dip and squeak with his weight as he sat down beside her. She regretted not pressing Regan for details about what would transpire this evening. It seemed rude to inquire about something so intimate between a man and woman, but not knowing what was expected of her was unsettling.

Grace was used to being in charge of her life. Hunter seemed to be usurping everything, including her peace of mind.

Her thoughts quieted at his touch.

Instead of tearing away the sheet and climbing on top of her like a mindless rutting beast, Hunter lightly brushed his thumb over her lower lip. Without thinking, she moistened her lips with her tongue and tasted the salty essence of his caress.

"Open your eyes."

Her eyelids lifted at his soft command. Hunter was leaning over her, his right arm keeping his weight off her. She had expected to see amusement in his expression, but the unguarded tenderness was a revelation.

"You have nothing to fear from me, Grace."

As if to prove his point, he lowered his head and lightly kissed her parted lips. This was not her first kiss. Lord Sey's youngest boy seized that honor when he pressed his advantage one autumn afternoon in the orchard as he planted a quick one on her lips.

She had been fourteen, and spent weeks fretting about her ardent companion's fate once the Duke of Huntsley learned of the incident. Of course, her concerns were unwarranted. The duke and his friends had been too busy scandalizing the *ton* to give a thought to his young betrothed.

Hunter paused, his mouth only an inch from hers. "A frown? That was not quite the response I had hoped to elicit."

Grace had not intended for her thoughts to wander, or for her husband to watch her so closely. Too many years had passed to allow an old disappointment to ruin a kiss she had been anticipating for most of her life. "On the contrary," she said, her lips molding into a rueful smile. "It was a lovely kiss."

He seemed to doubt her compliment. "Really?"

"Oh, most definitely," she hurriedly assured him. "One of the best I have ever experienced."

His eyes lit up with interest at her admission. "And how many rivals have sampled your sweet lips, Duchess?"

Grace casually shrugged. "I never bothered counting. Is the number important?" She widened her eyes and gazed innocently up at him.

He wondered if she was deliberately attempting to annoy him. "It might be," he grumbled. "If you are thinking of another gent when I have my hands on you."

"An impossibility, Your Grace," she assured him. "Dealing with you requires all of my wits."

Her answer pleased him. "Let's keep it that way, shall we?"

"And what of you?" she asked in a challenging tone. "Do you pine for another when you kiss me?"

Hunter gave her an impatient glance. "What are you implying, Duchess?"

"Nothing at all." She appeared to be mildly offended by his question. "I just want things to be fair between us. If I am not allowed to recall another gentleman's kiss, then the same rule applies to you as well."

Unused to having anyone dictate terms to how he lived his life, Hunter was not going to surrender his independence to a wife he never wanted in the first place. "And if I refuse?" he asked silkily.

"Then our wedding night will be rather uneventful," she said as she sat up, causing him to draw back. "For I refuse to share our marriage bed with another woman, especially with one who might have a special place in your heart."

A woman's logic, Hunter thought with frustration. At its core there was more heart than brain. Grace was less concerned with the notion that he had kissed other women than the thought that he might have held tender feelings for them.

Her concerns were utter nonsense since she had been the lady he had married.

"I see no other woman in this bed, but you," he said, striving for a soothing tone and likely failing. He had little experience in dealing with such trifles.

Most of his lovers would have never dared to complain or question him.

Grace had an annoying habit of challenging him.

It was maddening, but he could not say that his exchanges with his lady were boring.

"Now lie back down," Hunter said, gently easing her body back against the pillows. Her grip on the sheet was so fierce, he might have to tear the fabric to free her from her linen cocoon, but he would worry about it later. First, he needed her to relax. "There you go. What came before you can be left in the past, Duchess. Direct your thoughts to the present . . . to us."

Grace closed her eyes as he bent his head down to kiss her. Hunter was confident that she found him attractive. He had caught her studying him when she thought he wasn't paying attention. Lust was something he was intimately familiar with, and he could use it to shatter her defenses.

Her mouth felt stiff against his. She made no attempt to kiss him back, but he was undeterred. There had never been a female he could not seduce, and that included his reluctant bride.

"Are you chilled?" he asked, teasing the firm line of her mouth with his own.

"No," she replied, her lips parting as he had anticipated, and he did not hesitate to take advantage of the deliberate distraction.

Hunter captured her mouth, and kissed her. The tip of his tongue darted out to moisten and taste.

Her lips were as sweet as the wine she had imbibed at supper. He concentrated on her mouth, the softness of her plump lips, the flavor that was uniquely hers, and the faint stirring of her breath against his face.

"Open your mouth for me," he commanded, ignoring the husky urgency he detected in his voice.

Hunter preferred to take his time with a lover. Many gents rushed through the tender love play, their sole purpose focused on sticking their cocks into their willing partner. He understood their urgency. His unruly cock had become troublesome the moment he had entered the bedchamber to discover Grace sitting naked in the tub.

She tipped her face upward and parted her lips. He did not need any other encouragement. Gently he teased her mouth with his while his tongue brushed against her tongue, silently coaxing her to allow him entry. His wife was unused to passionate kissing. This delighted him for several reasons. First, it revealed that there was no secret beau waiting for her to return to the country. It also would give him the opportunity to instruct the fair lady in the art of kissing. If need be, he was prepared to dedicate hours to the pleasurable task.

Hunter cupped her chin with his thumb and first finger and leisurely stroked her face. "You taste like ambrosia," he murmured, indulging himself with another lingering kiss. "Now taste me. Use your tongue as I have."

He made a low sound of approval as the tip of her tongue glided over his teeth and rubbed against his. Encouraged by his response, she repeated the action, subtly widening her mouth as their tongues slowly entwined and danced.

With his eyes closed, he blindly slid his hand from the mattress to her left breast. Hunter could feel her taut nipple poking his palm through the thin barrier of the sheet. His cock ached at the knowledge that Grace was aroused by his kisses. He idly wondered if she was damp between her legs as well.

Soon he would have his answers, but he silently counseled himself to be patient. His duchess was no harlot or scheming mistress who thought only of the coin she'd gain by pleasuring him. For once, Hunter would have to work for his pleasure. The woman in his arms needed to be gently wooed. Her innocence was something to be treasured, and as much as he hungered for her, he wanted her to find some contentment in their coupling.

As far as Grace and Regan were concerned, Hunter had already made a hash of things by kidnapping his betrothed and bullying her into marrying him. He could set things right in their marriage bed. One might say, he had been practicing most of his life for this moment.

Hunter playfully squeezed her breast, causing Grace to face away and end their kiss.

"None of that," she said breathlessly. Their kissing had put color in her cheeks and the look was flattering. "It is unseemly—"

"For anyone to touch your breast," he spoke over her, sensing a lecture. "Anyone, that is, but me. I, however, may fondle your lovely breasts anytime it pleases me to do so, and now seems rather appropriate."

Eagerness ruined his good intentions as he strived for patience with his bride. Ignoring her protests, Hunter seized the edge of the sheet, and one abrupt tug bared her breast to his eager gaze.

"No, don't bother cover covering them," he said, lightly swatting aside her hands, though his eyes were focused on the bountiful display.

All laced tight within her stays, it had been difficult to deduce the plump flesh Grace had kept bound behind a cage of whalebone. Hunter cupped one of her breasts now, savoring the velvety feel of the warm flesh and the weight. He had never been particular when it came to the size or shape of a woman's breasts. Large or small, he had enjoyed fondling all of them.

Hunter admired the way her nipples tightened under his regard. A deep rosy pink, the sensitive flesh made him literally salivate at the thought of suckling them. In between her breasts, there was a light gold dusting of freckles. One, two, three, four . . . no five. He wondered what other surprises he would find as he explored his duchess's body.

"Beautiful."

Her eyes flew open at the sound of his voice. Before she could guess his intentions, Hunter leaned down and kissed one of her nipples.

"No!" she exclaimed as she tried to push him away.

Without looking up, he grabbed her wrists and pressed them into the pillows. His grip was firm, but he had no desire to hurt her. "Have a care, Duchess, I do not want to leave marks on your wrists."

"Then cease—"

She sucked in her breath when Hunter laved her nipple. A quick glance revealed that the tension in her arms had more to do with her fighting the new sensations he was creating within her than any attempt to free herself.

He shifted his attention to her other breast.

"Your Grace!"

Hunter smiled while he teased the swollen bud with his tongue. Taking a chance, he released her wrists, idly wondering if she would try to tear out his hair or box him on the ears now that she was free.

Grace did neither.

Instead she moved her arms from the pillows to the mattress. Her fingers dug into the thick padding as she shuddered. Hunter rubbed his lower lip against her nipple and raised his head while his fingers moved downward until they splayed across her both of her breasts.

"So you enjoy my caresses, eh?" he asked, not

expecting an honest response from her. "Let us see if I can change your sighs to cries of joy."

"Your Grace?"

"I keep telling you that Hunter will suffice, Duchess," he said, suddenly getting a mischievous look on his face. "You've earned the right. Or perhaps I might be able to persuade you into using my given name."

A look of panic crossed Grace's features. "No persuasion is necessary, Your Grace—Hunter!" she added hastily.

"Now you're just trying to spoil my fun," he teased, moving lower and taking the sheet she had drawn over her body with him.

"No . . . wait!"

The only thing Hunter was interested in prolonging was their mutual pleasure. Grace had already proven that she was responsive to his touch. He suspected fear more than aversion spurred her reluctance. If he was correct, then delaying the inevitable would be cruel.

He would claim her innocence, and then later they could figure out what sort of marriage they could build. Lust and attraction were poor materials for a solid foundation. Even so, it was more than either one of them had expected.

The sliding sheet revealed more of Grace's body. A delicate rib cage, the flat plains of her stomach with a delicate indentation Hunter longed to explore with his tongue.

Her entire body stiffened as his hands found the soft curves of her hips. "This is highly improper," she muttered, turning her head away as if she could not bear to witness what he planned to do next.

"Only if I do it right," he teased, but his bride failed to appreciate his humor. "And I promise, you will ask me to do this again."

Chapter Twenty-two

Grace had never felt so vulnerable in her life.

Never had a gentleman been permitted to caress her so boldly, and the Duke of Huntsley was proving to be quite thorough in his inspection of his latest acquisition. She refused to dress up her current circumstances with pretty lies. Nineteen years ago, Hunter's grandmother had conspired with her grandfather. She had cleverly figured out a way to do a favor for an old friend and expand her family's holdings. From all accounts, the old dowager had an analytic mind and a coldness to sacrifice anything and anyone to achieve her schemes.

Her grandson and Grace were suitable pawns.

She had been too young to understand and appreciate the dowager's Machiavellian efforts. However, her grandson had known. Was it any wonder that he had spent the past nineteen years pretending that he wasn't betrothed to a lady?

"Shift your leg," Hunter ordered, pressing a kiss to her bare hip bone. When she did not immediately comply, he placed his hand on her thigh and parted her legs.

Grace felt cool air between her legs as her husband's face hovered inches from a part of her body even she rarely gazed upon. The chill was an odd contrast with Hunter's breath, which was hot against her thigh.

"Artists would pay you a fortune to paint you thusly," Hunter said, his voice almost sounding reverent. His finger teased the hair nestled at the apex. "If such a painting existed, I would have it locked away in a private room for only my amusement."

Grace felt his thumb against the hair-covered folds between her legs.

Of all that is holy and sacred!

"Ask me what I would do in my private room?" he asked.

She gazed helplessly at the top of his head. His touch and scrutiny of the heart of her femininity was almost her undoing. She longed to push him away and cover herself with the sheet.

However, she was made of sterner stuff than that. Grace remained still as he stroked her, learning every line and contour of her body. It wasn't until he spoke again that she realized that she had yet to respond to his question.

"W-what would you do in this private chamber of yours, Your Grace?"

"Formality has no place in our bed, my lovely

duchess," he mildly rebuked as he tested a particularly sensitive spot just within her delicate folds.

Grace gasped at the sensation. "Stop that at once!" She slapped his shoulder to emphasis her point.

"I disagree," Hunter countered, raising his head until their gazes met. His light brown eyes gleamed like amber at her. "I do not wish to be indelicate, but you are wet."

Although her husband seemed quite pleased with his discovery, its significance meant little to her. "Of course I am wet, you lout! You dragged me out of a tub of water."

Grace had hoped to anger him enough that he would cease touching her so intimately. She could barely think with him making those tiny circles with his thumb.

Instead of being insulted, Hunter merely grinned at her. It was as if he knew exactly how she was feeling, and there was a good chance that he did. Thundering rake!

He gave her damp flesh a final caress before he held up his hand. "You believe this is water from your bath? No, my little innocent, this wetness is proof of your desire . . . for me," he said, practically purring the final two words.

Grace shook her head. "No. It isn't true. I am quite certain I abhor you."

Hunter snorted. "If this is abhorrence, we will get along famously." He placed his hand just below her breasts and gave her a gentle push. "Now behave yourself, and let me concentrate."

"Behave myself? Me?" She had done nothing to *him*.

"Yes, I know what I am asking is a trial for you."

Grace shivered as his damp fingers sought to test her sanity.

"However, if you behave, you shall learn that ceding to my instruction can be rewarding. Now close your eyes and stop arguing with me."

Grace complied, solely because she could not bear to watch. Oh, Hunter was not hurting her. It was quite the opposite, in fact. It amazed her that such large hands could be so gentle and teasing, and the sensations so intense. Her responses to his touch frightened her more than she could even admit to herself.

"And stop thinking," he muttered. "It only leads to trouble."

She opened her eyes and glared at him. "How do you know I'm thinking anything at all?"

He returned her angry stare with an exasperated look. "Your body stiffens whenever an unpleasant thought drifts through your head. Considering your current state, I'd wager it will take a raging bonfire to melt the iron in your bones."

"You consider this courting?"

"No, I call this bedding my wife," he replied, raising himself onto his elbows. "Are you planning to debate me the entire night?"

From his expression, Grace could tell that it might be prudent to remain silent. However, it just wasn't in her nature.

"You might want to summon the innkeeper for some wood."

Hunter appeared baffled by the change in subject. "And why would I want to do that?"

"Well, since you persist in being disagreeable, you might as well start building that bonfire," she said, reaching for the bedding he had pushed aside and pulling it over her breasts and abdomen. "I do not foresee me losing my stiffness."

Understanding flashed across his handsome face, and there was a hint of anger in his amber gaze before he groaned and allowed his forehead to connect with her upper thigh.

"With your sharp tongue, I can most certainly foresee the possibility."

"I beg your pardon?"

A heavy knock at the door startled them.

True to his name, Hunter's head snapped up. Absent was the man who took turns teasing and berating her. The intensity she noted on his face was different, almost predatory.

"Who—"

Hunter silenced her question with a gesture. He sat up and padded over to the door. "Who is it?" he demanded in a gruff voice.

"Forgive the intrusion, Your Grace." The man on the other side of the door sounded anxious. "You have a—a gentleman who insists on seeing you and—"

Hunter grimaced. "By God, if this is one of Frost's pranks, you can tell him to—"

"Oh, no, Your Grace," the innkeeper said, interrupting her husband's tirade. "It is, uh, another gentleman who requests an audience."

His mouth twisted with disdain. "At this late hour? I think not. Send the man away."

"Enough of this tomfoolery," a masculine voice interjected. "This is no way to run a respectable establishment. We tried it your way, now let us try mine. Huntsley, this is Strangham. I demand that you permit us entry, or I shall order my men to break down the door. The choice is yours."

"Is it, truly?"

Hunter cast a knowing smile at Grace. He had predicted that Strangham would attempt to prevent them from marrying, but she had not believed him. She clutched the sheet to her breasts while her gaze sought her discarded dress. Indecent hour or not, she had no intention of greeting her uncle and his companions attired only in a sheet.

"A moment if you please," he called out, gesturing for her to remain on the bed.

Naturally, Grace's instinct was to ignore her husband's command. She frantically tugged on her sheet to free it from the bedding, and her stance wobbled. If not for Hunter, she would have fallen flat onto her face.

Unmoved by either Strangham's threats or her panic, Hunter pressed a finger to his lips, signaling her silence. It took all of her discipline not to debate the issue, not to mention scream at him like an enraged harpy. When he was satisfied that she would obey his command, he kissed her on the forehead.

"Good girl. Stay here, and leave this to me, eh?" he whispered in her ear.

Before she could reply, Hunter left her and walked over to the table where a bowl of fruit was displayed. He retrieved a small knife from the wooden bowl and returned to her side.

She glanced at the knife in his hand, and then met his steady gaze. "Murdering the bride on her wedding night. I thought such tales were only found in epic poems and novels."

"Is that what you've filled your head with, Duchess? Gothic tales of romance and murder?"

"Of course not," she said too quickly.

"Don't fret, love," he replied, raising the knife. "The blade is for me, not you."

Good grief, he did not intend to—"I beg of you, do not!"

Hunter drew the blade over his first two fingers. A thin line of blood welled in the cut. He squeezed the self-inflicted wound until he was satisfied with the amount of blood.

Meanwhile, her uncle had ordered the innkeeper to pound on the door. Whatever Hunter's plan, he needed to execute it swiftly.

"What are you about, Your Grace?" she asked in hushed tones.

"Claiming your virginity," he said simply. He moved by her and smeared the blood across the sheet covering the mattress. "And I will paddle your backside if you utter anything to the contrary to our unwelcome visitors."

He spoke his threat so mildly, but she had no doubt he would deliver a punishment for any interference on her part.

"Huntsley!"

Without asking for permission, he swept her up into his arms and placed her on the bed. "There . . . delightfully mussed, but one thing is missing."

She glanced down at her front, and then glared at him. "Yes, that would be my clothing."

Hunter chuckled. He probably thought it was amusing that she was sitting naked in their bed with the wolves at the door.

"No, this."

Before she could try her next breath, his mouth was covering her and he was kissing her with a ferocity that wiped all thoughts from her head. Gone was the patient coaxing her into accepting his kisses. Hunter took what was rightfully his. Her vision narrowed as his tongue ravished her mouth with delicious and rough thoroughness.

When they pulled apart, Grace's lips were slightly swollen and there were fading marks where he had gripped her by the arms.

"An improvement," he said, with a studious nod of his head. "Now remember what I said. It might be best if you let me do all the talking."

He swaggered away to confront their visitors, and that was when she noticed the red scratches on his back. Had she blindly marred his flesh? She was too appalled to say another word. Instead she slid off the mattress and headed for her discarded chemise. She pulled the undergarment over her head and practically dove for the covers when she realized Hunter had no intention of waiting for her to dress.

He opened the door and glowered at the small crowd that had assembled in front of the room. "Strangham, I would like to say this is most unexpected, but I did not take you to be gracious in your disappointment. Otherwise, we might have invited you to the wedding."

Grace wondered if anyone would mind if she pulled the bedding over her head and waited for everyone to leave. She could not fathom why Hunter even bothered to open the door at all. The entire situation was humiliating and intolerable. She pulled the bedding higher.

Her uncle's entire body trembled in fury. He stabbed a finger at Hunter. "I want this man arrested for kidnapping my niece. Summon the magistrate."

Uncertain, the stocky innkeeper glanced fretfully at Hunter. He did not want to offend the duke, but her uncle's accusations were troubling.

"Strangham, cease these melodramatics. You are

worrying our good host. Is that not right, Hopkins?"
Hunter said, not taking his hardened gaze off her
uncle.

"I beg your pardon, Your Grace, for disturbing
your sleep," the innkeeper said.

"Think nothing of it, my good man," Hunter said
genially. "As one can expect from a newly married
gent, I was not asleep." He winked at their visitors.

His meaning could not be any clearer to anyone
within earshot. Several men chuckled at Hunter's
ribald comment. Grace's face flamed with heat.

Only her uncle seemed to be more outraged than
her. "You took the girl by force, you blackguard!" he
seethed. "I have it on good authority that once my
niece had been removed from your questionable influence, she had no intention of marrying you."

"A lover's tiff, Strangham," Hunter said dismissively. "If you ever manage to convince a woman to
unfasten your trousers you might discover that females can be rather disagreeable creatures when provoked."

"Blame the woman. Such a typical remark from a
man," grumbled Grace. Her eyes widened and she
brought her hand to her unruly mouth when she noticed that everyone was staring at her.

"Eyes on me, gents," Hunter said sharply. "That is
my *wife* all of you are ogling."

Chapter Twenty-three

"How rude of you, Hunter, to throw a private gathering, and forget to invite your friends," Frost drawled, drawing everyone's attention away from Grace.

She had never felt so grateful.

Hunter snorted. "Stay away from my duchess, Frost. And you can blame Strangham for disturbing the entire inn. Thinks he's rescuing his niece from my evil clutches or some rot."

"How dare you make a mockery of my concerns!" Strangham roared.

"It appears the bride prefers to remain in your evil clutches, Hunter," Frost observed drily.

Grace noticed that Dare and Regan were also present. She rested her forehead onto her knees, which she had drawn to her chest. Frost was correct. This evening was turning into some kind of untoward gathering. All they needed was food and drink.

Grace began to giggle.

"Let me through," Regan said, pushing her way through. "Can't you see that all of you are terrifying the Duke of Huntsley's bride?" The crowd parted, allowing her to march up to Hunter. She halted and glared up at him. "I will tend to your wife while you—" She gestured wildly at the group of men. "—handle this."

Her uncle turned on Regan. "My niece does not need assistance from one of the inn's doxies."

Grace lifted her face from her knees. Hunter, Dare, and Frost each took an intimidating step toward her uncle. As Frost's sister, Regan had been doted on by all of the Lords of Vice. She knew that Hunter looked upon Dare's wife as a little sister. Insulting her might be her uncle's undoing.

"See to Grace," Hunter murmured to Regan as he stepped around her.

Dare's large hand landed on her uncle's shoulder. He must have tightened his grip, because the other man winced. "You are quick with the accusations, Strangham. How are you with apologies? The lady you casually insulted is the Marchioness of Pashley. She also happens to be my wife, you arse!"

"Perhaps you do not remember me, Strangham," Frost said in icy tones. "I am Chillingsworth. Regan is my sister. If you are done pestering my friend and his bride, perhaps you have time to offer us the names of your seconds." He glanced at Dare. "As always, I offer my services as your second."

Dare turned her uncle around to address the mess he had created by insulting Regan. To Frost he said,

"While I would prefer to tear this gentleman's limbs off with my bare hands, your assistance is welcome."

Regan retrieved a shawl from one the chairs and wrapped it around Grace's shoulders. "All will be well," she whispered. "It is best to let the men handle this."

Her uncle had managed to infuriate three Lords of Vice. He was fortunate the other four had not joined them on their journey.

"See here . . . I meant no disrespect to your lady." Strangham nodded to Frost. "Your sister. Please accept my apologies. I confess, I have not quite been myself since I was told that Huntsley had kidnapped my niece."

"Someone lied to you," Frost said flatly.

"Lady Grace was among friends. She was never in any danger," Dare added. His expression revealed that he was still not satisfied with her uncle's apology.

Grace was impressed that both men could lie so convincingly. Regan touched her on the arm. A subtle warning to remain silent about the truth about her elopement. As upset as she was with Hunter, she had no intention of leaving the inn with her uncle.

"Check with the priest if you do not believe us," Hunter said, recapturing Strangham's attention. "Grace is my wife. She came to my bed willingly and the sheets bear proof of the consummation."

"Merciful heavens."

Grace brought her hands up to her face. Hunter

had just announced that he had taken her virginity. Her cheeks felt as if they had been scalded with boiling water.

"I demand to see this proof," her uncle demanded.

A strangled gasp escaped her lips. "No!"

Hunter glanced back at her. His enigmatic expression gave no hint as to what he wanted from her. "Strangham, you have upset my wife. How many challenges do you intend to collect from the Lords of Vice this evening?"

The innkeeper stepped between the two gentlemen before her uncle could reply. "With the priest confirming the validity of the marriage, one witness should suffice. Lady Pashley, if you do not mind, could you examine the sheets?"

"Of course. If it will put an end to the matter," Regan said, giving Grace an encouraging smile. "With your permission, Your Grace."

Grace shifted her wary gaze to her uncle. She did not fully understand her uncle's motives, but she doubted he had developed a sudden affection for her. Neither had Hunter, for that matter. The duke and Strangham were like two feral mongrels fighting over a bone.

It was an unsavory position when one was the bone.

"Is this necessary?" Grace said to no one in particular, though her steady gaze remained on her husband. He'd told her to let him handle their unwelcome guests, but a public viewing of the bed linens was too much, even if very little had transpired in the bed.

"Do not fret, Duchess," Hunter said with false cheerfulness. "One witness will suffice. Regan, if you please."

With a soft huff of annoyance, Grace shifted and pulled back the sheet so Regan could see the smear of blood Hunter had placed upon the sheet. Regan peered at the blood. At a distance, the men craned their necks to get a glimpse of the sheets. Fortunately, her husband's indomitable presence was enough to keep the crowd from crossing the threshold.

"Regan?" Hunter prompted.

Regan lifted her gaze to study Grace. "Are you well?"

It took a moment for her to understand what her new friend was asking. Regan wanted to know if Hunter had hurt her.

Grace shook her head. "I am fine. It is kind of you to inquire," she whispered, embarrassed that everyone knew what Hunter had supposedly done to her in this bedchamber, when she only could only speculate with her limited knowledge.

Regan nodded as she dropped the sheet. She turned to face the waiting group of men. "Wondrous news, Your Grace." She addressed Strangham directly. "I can assure you that adding your congratulations to the happy, and most definitely married couple will be the swiftest way for you to excuse yourself, and not humiliate yourself more than you have."

Strangham was unused to being dismissed by anyone. He pointed a finger at Grace. "Now, see here."

"What I see is a gentleman who cannot accept the truth," Hunter said, pinning him with a hard stare. "The lady is mine. She was placed in my care when she was a child, and I have honored the terms of the marriage contract set forth by my grandmother and her grandfather by making her my wife. This business is done. Take your leave, Strangham."

"Perhaps the gent requires some assistance," Frost said, his unusual turquoise-blue eyes staring at the older duke as if measuring him for a shroud.

Outnumbered, her uncle should have accepted his defeat and departed. Unfortunately, he proved to be exceedingly stubborn when cornered. "I have not heard from my niece. Perhaps she might offer a differing opinion about these hasty nuptials."

The room grew silent, and all eyes shifted to the silent figure huddled on the bed. Hunter, Dare, Frost, and Regan appeared to be particularly tense as everyone waited for her to respond. And why should they not? After all, she had been kidnapped by the four of them, while Hunter spent the journey alternating between cajoling and bullying her into marrying him. One word and she could ruin what was left of their wedding night.

Of course, it would not make me any less married to the rogue!

And Hunter would find a way to punish her for such mischief. Grace cleared her throat and strived for as much dignity as she could muster as she sat dressed in her chemise and wrapped like a cocooned caterpillar in the bed linens.

"Uncle, I do not know who was whispering in your ear, but they filled your head with lies. I willingly married the Duke of Huntsley."

Strangham's shoulders sagged at her announcement, but his expression was filled with impotent fury as he glared at her. "With all of this excitement, perhaps it has slipped you mind, dear niece. You caused quite a stir when you arrived in London. The *ton* was agog when it was rumored that you sought to marry someone other than Huntsley."

Well, he had a point. After Hunter's neglect, she had thought any gentleman would suffice. Grace shrugged. "I was annoyed with Hunter. It was petty, but I sought to make him jealous."

"You succeeded," muttered Hunter.

Her uncle gave her a look of disbelief. "The man neglected you for years . . . betrayed you with countless women."

Hunter stirred from his rigid stance. "You go too far, Strangham."

Grace could not conceal her wince. She felt sick inside, knowing her uncle was not embellishing the truth.

"I think His Grace has said enough," Dare said, preparing to drag her uncle bodily from the inn in order to spare him from the pummeling Hunter was preparing to deliver.

"My lords, please," the innkeeper pleaded, franticly gesturing for all of them to remain civil in his establishment. "We have established that the Duke of Huntsley did not kidnap his intended, and the marriage is valid. My apologies for disturbing you and your duchess, Your Grace." He inclined his head in Grace's direction. "Madam."

Hunter clapped his hand onto the innkeeper's shoulder. His benevolent smile was not fooling anyone. "Quite understandable, Hopkins, what with strangers rushing into the inn in the middle of the night with wild tales of a kidnapping."

"You are being generous, Your Grace," the innkeeper said, his gaze shifting to the gentleman who had caused all the trouble.

"You are apologizing to *him*? What about *me*? He's not telling you the entire story," Strangham muttered, even though he was being escorted away by the innkeeper and his servant. Dare and Frost were close on their heels in case her uncle resisted. "Somehow they have convinced my niece to lie on their behalf."

"There, there, Your Grace," Hopkins said in soothing tones he reserved for agitated aristocrats. "Take heart in knowing your niece has married well, and there's no shame to the family name."

Her uncle sounded like he was choking on his outrage. "This isn't finished, Huntsley!" he said through clenched teeth.

"I'll accept your challenge any day you have the

courage to issue it," Hunter replied, raising his hand in farewell.

Frost, who was about to walk away, halted and scowled at his friend. "You might want to bandage that small wound on your hand," he said when Strangham could no longer overhear them. "Wouldn't want it to fester, now, would we? In fact, I'd see to that task straightaway." His gaze drifted to Grace. His meaning was all too clear.

He was aware that Hunter had not bedded Grace.

"Your advice is duly noted," Hunter said, inclining his head. "And Frost?"

The earl glanced at him expectantly. "Yes."

Hunter braced his hand on the door frame, blocking the other man's view of Grace. "If you and Dare cannot encourage Strangham to leave the inn, I would appreciate it if you could keep him from disturbing us again."

Frost sighed. "The petite brunette I have waiting in my bed will be disappointed. Nevertheless, I can postpone my casual amusements for another night."

"Thank you. I knew I could count on you."

With a wave of farewell, Hunter shut the door. He leaned against it and crossed his arms.

"As amusing as that was, this was not how I intended to spend my wedding night."

Chapter Twenty-four

Hunter stuck his head in the doorway. "The horses and coach are waiting. Are you ready to leave this hospitable inn?"

It had been a long night, and she did not have the fortitude to poke the beast. "Yes, of course." Grace bent down and checked the position of her bonnet in the small mirror the innkeeper's wife had provided. Satisfied, she tied her ribbons and picked up the small satchel that had been left behind at her request.

Regan had gone to the trouble of packing a few items she thought Grace would require for her wedding journey. It was a sweet gesture, and one she could appreciate even if the outing had begun with trickery. She did not blame the young marchioness, who was eager to return to her infant son, for her part in Grace's kidnapping.

She blamed Hunter.

The man had been determined to have his way, and was ruthless and cunning enough to claim what and whom he wanted.

"Carrying your own bags?" Frost said, coming up from behind her. "This will not do."

She surrendered the small satchel, understanding that Hunter was not the only one who believed everyone should bow to his dictates. It was something all seven Lords of Vice had in common.

"Did you get any sleep?" she asked, stifling a yawn.

"Enough. I can always sleep in the coach if the night catches up with me." Frost had recently bathed and looked quite alert for a gentleman who had stayed up all night.

It was then that she realized his sudden appearance was no accident. He had been waiting for her to emerge from the room she had shared with Hunter.

"What about you, Duchess? Did you get some rest?"

Grace glanced at him, wondering if he was inquiring about the details of her wedding night with Hunter. There was nothing in his expression to suggest that his question was unseemly so she answered him truthfully.

"I am unused to sleeping in an inn. The sounds beyond the door kept disturbing my sleep. There were times when I thought my uncle had returned."

She had not been the only one who had not slept well. Hunter had heard those same noises. On each occasion, the arm he had draped across her waist tensed as he listened keenly for any sign of trouble.

"With the exception of the coachman, it appears

our journey home will be a peaceful one," he said a little too cheerfully.

So she had been a little upset on the way to Gretna Green. Was it her fault that she had been drugged and kidnapped by Hunter? Blistering his ears with her displeasure had been the least he deserved.

"I would not place a wager on that prediction," she replied sweetly as they walked across the yard toward their coach. "I may have married Hunter, but time will tell if our union is a reward or a punishment."

Frost chuckled. "Darling, if I could have stolen you away from Hunter I would have. You remind me so much of another lady I worship."

"Ignore my brother, Grace," Regan said, poking her head in the doorway. She and Dare had already settled into their seats. "Frost worships no one but himself."

"You wound me, sister. I love easily."

"Too easily," Dare concurred. "Just ask the brunette who emerged from his room this morning."

Regan snuggled up to her husband and laid her cheek against his shoulder. "You forgot about the blonde."

Grace looked askance at Frost.

He tried to look repentant but utterly failed at the task. "Mere shadows of the lady whom I worship as my sun."

"Are you still trying to seduce my wife, Frost?"

Hunter walked around from the back of the coach. For a man who wondered if he was being cuckolded, he seemed rather calm about it.

"If I had, there would have been no *trying* involved." He winked at Grace. "I would have succeeded."

Hunter came up to Grace. Neither one of them knew what to expect from the other, which made her feel awkward. Her husband slipped his arm around her waist and pulled her against him. "Morning, Duchess." He kissed her on the mouth, staking his claim.

Perhaps Frost's teasing comments had goaded Hunter to make a very public declaration.

"Good morning, husband," she murmured when he released her. She climbed into the coach before he could reach for her again.

It seemed as if they had been sitting in the coach for half the day when Regan had grumbled to everyone awake that they should have packed a chamber pot for the trip. Hunter got the hint. He rapped on the trapdoor and ordered the coachman to halt.

They were supposed to stop to water the horses, and the area provided enough trees for privacy.

"Walk with me, Grace," Regan said, necessity quickening her stride.

Grace glanced back as she followed the marchioness into the copse. Hunter stood near the horses as he quietly spoke with the coachman. Frost and Dare were heading in the opposite direction. Regan was not the only one who was yielding to bodily needs.

Grace headed deeper into the thicket. Grimacing at their rustic conditions, she quickly emptied her bladder while she struggled to maintain her dignity and keep the hem of her skirt dry.

"Are you still there," Regan called out.

"Yes." Until she had traveled to London, she had not understood how solitary her life had been. Now she could not take a brief stroll in the woods without tripping over someone.

"What are you grinning about? Did you find an old frog to kiss?" Regan teased.

"Frost has already stolen a kiss," Grace replied in kind, but faltered at her friend's expression. It was easy to forget that Regan and Frost were brother and sister.

"My brother did *what*?"

"It was a jest," she lied. Even when she blurted out the confession to Hunter that first night, he had not believed her. There was no reason to stir up trouble for the earl over a harmless flirtation. "Shall we head back?"

"One more thing before we return to the coach." Regan sobered. "I did not have a chance to ask earlier. Are you well? It was your wedding night and I—" She grimaced. "Truth be told, I am feeling quite awkward for even asking, but I was worried about you . . . and Hunter, though he does not deserve it."

Touched by the woman's concern, Grace fought back the urge to cry. Naturally, Regan presumed the worst. "Oh, no," she said with a watery smile. "I am fine. I lost my mother so long ago, it just occurred to me that this is something she might have asked me."

"I doubt it," Regan instantly replied.

Grace laughed. "You are probably correct. Still, you are considerate to inquire after my welfare." She inhaled, wondering if she should tell her friend the truth. Too embarrassed to utter the words out loud, she beckoned Regan closer and whispered in her ear. "I am . . . Hunter did not."

"Are you certain?" Regan whispered back, her eyes round with disbelief.

"Of course I am," she replied. "I may have been sheltered, but I think I would have recognized that Hunter and I . . ." She was incapable of finishing the sentence.

Thankfully, Regan understood. "Well, why not? What's wrong with the gent?"

"Nothing!" she replied, slightly offended on Hunter's behalf. Before her uncle's arrival, her husband had seemed quite willing to seduce her. "With the possibility of Strangham lurking about, Hunter thought more about protecting me than pleasuring himself."

Or her.

After everyone had left, he had gotten into the bed with her and ordered her to go to sleep. At first, she had felt relief for the reprieve he had granted her.

As the minutes ticked by, doubt had begun to creep into her thoughts. What if Hunter had regretted marrying her? Through no fault of her own, she came with a troubled past. Perhaps Strangham's appearance reminded her husband of that fact.

A soft sound of distress vibrated in her throat at the thought. Hunter had misunderstood the reasons for it, but he had reached for her with the intent of soothing her. Tenderly he had curled himself around her, and wrapped his arm around her waist. His hand brushed her breast, but it must have been an accident.

"Go to sleep," he had murmured sleepily into her ear.

Grace had been comforted by the heat of his body and the strength of his arms around her. Gradually, she had managed to drift off to sleep. Well, until the sounds of the night had disturbed their light slumber.

"Although it is quite unlike him, I believe Hunter was being considerate to your feelings," Regan said as she mulled over what Grace had told her. "Wait until I tell Dare."

Grace paled at the thought. She frantically shook her head. "No, you cannot tell anyone what I told you. His friends—"

"What are you two whispering about?" Hunter demanded.

Grace and Regan were so startled, they screamed. She clapped her hand over her mouth. Her friend slapped Hunter on the arm.

"Beast! You frightened us half to death," Regan said, stalking by him with her head held high.

"Difficult female. How does Dare tolerate your surly disposition in the morning?" Hunter called after her.

"He does not make the mistake of frightening me while I'm indisposed," was her reply.

"Did I say anything to offend her?" he asked Grace.

"I think she is still cross with you for tricking us into journeying to Gretna Green," she said, unwilling to admit the true direction of their conversation.

"Hell and damnation!" Hunter removed his hat and slapped it against his thigh. "You and Regan may be insulted by high-handed method, but the reasons for it were sound. Strangham's arrival is proof enough."

Hunter was correct, though she loathed to admit it. She'd had no inkling that her uncle would pursue them. "Your Grace, I—"

Her husband hissed and reached for his shoulder. Before she could inquire after his odd reaction, he tackled her to the ground.

She gasped as she felt his full weight. "I cannot breathe, you oaf. Let me up!"

"Stay down," he growled, as he searched what he could see of the horizon.

"What is wrong?" It was then that she noticed that his frock coat was torn at the shoulder and the fabric was wet. "Good grief, you are bleeding!"

"Stop fussing and stay still," he commanded when she tried to inspect the damage. "Someone shot at us, and I would prefer that we do not present him with another target."

"You were shot?"

"Not really," he said, smiling down at her. "The bastard missed."

"Hunter?"

Grace recognized Frost's voice. Relieved he was unharmed, she struggled to sit up, but Hunter held her in place.

"I have Grace. Where is Regan?" Hunter called out.

"With Dare. They were near the coach when all of us heard the weapon discharge."

Grace heard the earl's footfalls as he approached them. She had to peer over her husband's shoulder to get a glimpse of the man. He had a pistol in his hand. "The coachman and I searched the surrounding area. Whoever it was, he appears to have scurried off like a rat. A startled hunter, you think?"

Hunter rolled off her, giving her a chance to catch her breath.

"He has been shot," she said, earning an inscrutable look from her husband.

"Shot?" Frost said, crouching down beside them, his brow furrowed with concern. "How bad is it?"

Hunter winced at his friend's touch. "The bullet grazed my shoulder when I took a step toward—"

His implication was obvious.

"Me?" she squeaked. "Are you suggesting that someone was shooting at me?"

His fierce expression eased. "Not at all. It was likely a hunter who was unaware that we were on his land."

"Aye, a hunter," Frost said, supporting his friend.

Grace began to shiver. One thing was certain. Neither man could lie very well.

Hunter believed her uncle was behind their mishap.

Chapter Twenty-five

A week later, after their adventurous journey back to London, Hunter and Grace were the guests of honor at the Sainthills' residence. There had been several balls held in their honor since their return. London society was thrilled that another Lord of Vice had succumbed to love, and everyone wanted to be introduced to the new Duchess of Huntsley.

The *ton* adored her.

Grace was equally flattered and overwhelmed by all of the attention. Hunter tried to assure her that he did not care what those fawning sycophants thought of their marriage, but his attempts to ease her fears only seemed to put more distance between them.

His duchess might be heralded as the darling of polite society, but he was a dismal failure as a husband. A part of him wanted to blame Strangham, but it had taken him days before he could acknowledge the truth staring him in the face. Hunter had taken the steps to ensure that Grace was bound to him legally. He had overlooked something more important—her heart.

Grace was not in love with him.

Nor had she forgiven him for his callous abandonment and disregard for her tender feelings.

Hunter recognized the signs. Over the years, he had bedded too many ladies who were unhappy with their lives. They had turned to him to briefly assuage the emptiness, and he had been content to provide the brief amusement that they craved.

He had not loved any of them. Even his feelings for Portia paled in comparison with what he felt for Grace.

Hunter had fallen in love.

He could almost hate her for it.

Saint placed a companionable arm around Hunter. "How is the shoulder?"

"Healing, or else I would be howling in pain. Your fingers are digging into the wound."

He grinned at his friend's hasty withdrawal.

"My apologies," Saint said, shaking his head. "I can't decide if you are extremely lucky or courting misfortune. Christ, Hunter, that hunter could have put a hole in your skull."

Hunter raised his glass of wine. "Since I'd like to keep my head in one piece, I am viewing myself as very fortunate." The two men clicked their glasses together. "What gives me nightmares is Grace. She could have been struck down."

If the shooting had been deliberate, she could have

been the man's target instead of some meandering deer. Since his return, he had hired a Bow Street Runner to look into Strangham's whereabouts. The duke had not returned to London, or so it appeared. Hunter wanted to know where to find the man, and ask him a few questions.

He was not particular on how he obtained his answers, either.

As if sensing his dark thoughts, Grace glanced in his direction. She was seated between Catherine and Isabel. All of the Lords of Vice were in attendance, including their wives. Together they were the family both he and Grace had been denied because of tragedy. As he observed her laugh at something Reign said, his heart ached. He should have invited her into his life years ago.

"Come."

Hunter blinked. He and Saint had separated themselves from the others, choosing to observe rather than participate. "Where are we going?"

"To find something stronger in my library," Saint said, leaving the decision for Hunter to remain or follow in his hands.

He decided to join his friend.

Grace was surrounded by his friends. She would not miss him for a few minutes if he and Saint lingered downstairs.

Saint was pouring brandy into the glasses when he entered the library. "There you are. I wondered if you might spare me."

Confused, Hunter asked, "Spare you from what precisely?"

Saint rubbed his neck as if it pained him. "I lost the draw, and have been elected to speak to you privately."

Well, this was news.

"About what?"

"Your marriage," he said bluntly. "Or should I say, your marriage in name only to Grace."

"Christ, who told you?" Hunter demanded.

"Does it matter?" Saint countered. "Never mind who told me. You already gave yourself away with your response."

He swallowed the brandy, savoring the burn as the liquid coursed down his throat. The action prevented him from saying something he would likely regret.

"It is not my place to pry into your private life."

"But you intend to do it anyway" was Hunter's dry reply.

"Look, I am as uncomfortable as you are, but you have us concerned," Saint replied, his voice infused with love and sincerity that it was difficult to be angry with his interference. "Strangham is missing. Your cousin has been moping about London since the news of your elopement. Do you want to be responsible for cheering him up?"

"Hell, no," Hunter protested. "I had hoped he had given up by now."

"He hasn't," Saint informed him. "If he learns your marriage has not been consummated and Grace is still angry enough at you to demand an annulment . . . well, my friend, then you have a problem."

Hunter took another sip and leaned against the edge of the desk. "It is complicated."

"Is it, uh, physical?"

It took a moment for Hunter to figure out what Saint was talking about. "No!" he said harshly. "I do not require any special treatments for my condition if that's what you are asking."

Oh, hell, maybe he should find Grace and just leave before this conversation became any more awkward.

"Then is it Grace?" Saint asked tentatively. He sensed he was treading on uncertain territory. "Has she barred you from her bedchamber?"

Hunter thought of their wedding night. Grace had been naked and willing after a little coaxing from him. He ached for her each night, but he wanted to give her time to accept the marriage he had tricked and bullied her into accepting.

"I can't do this, Saint." Hunter shook his head. "You won't understand. I love her and I don't . . ." He trailed off as he noted his friend's slack-jawed expression. "Forget it."

"I don't believe it. You have fallen in love with Grace."

How could he deny it?

"Yes," Hunter said, feeling liberated by his confession. "It's either love or madness. Personally, I was leaning toward madness."

Saint laughed. "I am intimately familiar with your

internal struggle, my friend. For six years, you and the others watched me as I battled myself and Catherine. Neither one of us wanted to fall in love."

"Do you have any regrets?"

"No," Saint said without any hesitation. "What about you?"

Hunter wearily sighed. "I have nineteen of them."

"Do you want some advice?"

He could not believe he was willing to listen to Saint as he lectured him on the subject of love. "Not particularly, but I have a feeling you are planning to offer it anyway."

"Forget about your mistakes. Bed your duchess."

"To fulfill the terms of the contract," Hunter said, cursing his grandmother for meddling beyond the grave. "Because that is exactly what Grace will believe if I bed her."

"The marriage was set up to protect her from Strangham," Saint reminded him. "Honor your commitment to her by giving her your body."

"What if I wish to offer her more?"

"Then give yourself and Grace a chance to figure out what this marriage could mean to both of you. Your self-imposed celibacy is admirable, but you are denying your nature. Do all of us a favor and bed your wife. Trust me, the rest has a way of working itself out."

Hours later, Grace sat at her dressing table brushing her hair. The maid had already undressed her and

taken down her hair. Dressed in her white nightgown, she looked virginal. It did not escape her notice that she was a married virgin, something she
had never expected when she was married to a Lord
of Vice.

Perhaps even a notorious rake had his limits, she
thought darkly.

She was married to a gentleman who could not
stomach bedding her. Any gentle overtures had been
politely rebuffed, she assumed for the sake of appearances; Hunter came to her bedchamber each
evening. He carried her to bed, held her in his arms,
and kissed her sweetly on the lips as if she were
something to be treasured.

Some nights he remained and she slept contently
in his embrace. In the morning, when she awoke he
was gone. Then there were the nights she reached
for him, silently entreating him to truly make her his
wife. Those were the nights she had learned to
loathe. Instead of accepting her invitation, he made
some pathetic excuse to leave her. She spent those
nights crying herself to sleep.

In a moment of weakness, she had confessed her
frustrations to Regan. The marchioness had held her
while she had sobbed, and then ordered her to dry
her tears. They had spent the next few hours conspiring on ways to break through Hunter's resistance.

Nothing had worked.

There was a familiar knock at the door.

Hunter. He had decided to come to her after all.

"You may enter," she called out, though her invitation was unnecessary. Her husband came and went from her life as he pleased.

"I trust you had a good evening at the Sainthills?" Grace politely asked, noting her husband had retired for the evening and wore his favorite blue silk dressing gown.

"I did. Catherine is quite inventive when it comes to games." He kissed her on the cheek. "The lady never disappoints her guests."

Gently he removed the brush from her hand, and began sliding it through her hair. She had worked through all the knots, so the brush glided effortlessly through her tresses. It surprised her that he enjoyed the menial task, but he seemed fascinated with her hair.

"You and Saint vanished for an hour," she said, already regretting that she had called attention to his disappearance.

"Hmm."

When he did not elaborate, she pressed, "Where did you go?"

"The library. The Sainthills stock an excellent wine, but I prefer brandy. Saint invited me downstairs to share a glass or two."

"Ah, I see." She did not know what else to say. Each day, the distance between them expanded. Perhaps her uncle had been correct, after all. Now that Hunter had laid claim to her fortune, he had little use for her, except to beget his heir.

Even in this she was a failure.

Her lower lip traitorously quivered. She bit her lip to hide her misery from her husband.

Hunter placed the brush on the dressing table beside the matching comb of ivory and silver. "The hour is late, Duchess. Come to bed."

Grace rose from the small bench and placed her hand in his. He escorted her to the bed as if they were preparing to dance. She wondered what he would do if she curtsied before him.

"Remove your nightgown."

The command was so unexpected, she just gaped at him.

Instead of asking her again, Hunter grabbed the hem and pulled it over her head. He let the garment drop at his feet.

"What are you about, husband?"

He offered her a slight knowing smile. It was the one that used to annoy her when she first met him.

"A new game I wish to play."

He shrugged out of his dressing gown. The silk caressed his body as it slipped to the floor. Gloriously naked, there was no concealing the fact that he was fully aroused. His manhood jutted proudly between his legs.

Grace moistened her lips with her tongue.

"What do you call this game?"

"It doesn't have a name," he confessed rather sheepishly. "I am making it up as I go along. Perhaps you can assist me in giving it a proper name."

He swept her up into his arms and carried her to the bed. Without any clothing to shield his gaze, her first inclination was to cover her breasts.

However, the few steps it took to carry her to the bed prevented her from recovering her modesty. Hunter placed her on the bed. She reached for the sheet, but he stopped her.

"Indulge me, Duchess. I have often thought of our wedding night and wondered if it were all a dream."

Had Regan told Hunter of her longings? No, she could not imagine the marchioness breaking her oath. However, something in her husband's demeanor had changed.

He gave her a gentle push to encourage her to lie on her back. His hands slid from her shoulders and down over her breasts. His thumbs stroked her nipples until they hardened and ached. Hunter was far from finished. He leaned over her, his thick arousal brushing her knee.

"Have I mentioned how torturous it's been each night to hold you?" he asked, his hungry gaze lingering on her nipples.

"N—no," she stammered, fighting back the urge to cry.

Her tears were not of sorrow, but of joy.

Hunter had decided not to deny either one of them any longer.

"Each night I conjure your naked form in my mind. In meticulous detail, I have orchestrated each tantalizing stroke with my hands, my tongue and lips, and my cock. It pleases me that your beauty exceeds the limits of my imagination."

Grace glanced at this magnificently male specimen and was breathless with the realization that he belonged to her. "I would return the compliment by touching you as well, Your Grace."

"Not yet, my impatient wench," he said, chastising her lightly by molding his fingers around her hips and squeezing, before moving down to her thighs. "I will not last if you put your hands on me."

"Hunter. Stop. I do not understand," she said when he parted her thighs. "Why are you doing this? I thought you no longer desired me."

He stilled at her accusation.

His amber eyes blazed with the flame of lust and anger. "Not desire you? Duchess, I burn each night for you. Alone, I stroke myself in private, longing for your hands to bring me to completion. Not want you? Denying myself has brought on a fever that dreams along cannot quench."

"Hunter." She whispered his name in growing wonderment.

"Well, no longer. I have grown weary of waiting for you to forgive me," he said huskily. "I will deny myself not a minute longer."

Without warning, he buried his face between her legs. His fingers parted the soft folds and his mouth unerringly found the delicate flesh within.

Grace instinctively reached for Hunter, her fingers threading though his hair. She moaned as he tasted her. He stroked her with his tongue, over and over, until she fell back against the mattress and surrendered to his lovemaking. Her thighs trembled and her entire body ached as he continued his tender assault to her senses.

The dampness between her legs increased, but any embarrassment was banished by her husband's growl of pleasure. He savored the taste of her, and the response of her body.

She gasped, feeling a flutter of sensation across her pelvis as her womb tightened in anticipation. Hunter raised his head, his gaze glowing with satisfaction and anticipation.

Chapter Twenty-six

"Your desire is sweet and thick as honey on my tongue," Hunter said, rising to give her full view of his arousal. It was a magnificent display of virility. One he intended to put to good use, he mused, as he crawled up her body and used his hand to position that rigid length against her womanly folds.

"I have bedded many women, Grace," he admitted, gazing longingly into her beautiful face. "However, this will be a first for me."

Not giving Grace a chance to question him further, Hunter guided his cock, rubbing the thick head against the drenched folds, teasing the small knot of flesh within until she writhed against him. He squeezed the rigid flesh in his grasp, striving to control his responses.

It was obvious his duchess was unaware how much he craved her. Saint was correct. He had waited long enough to claim his wife. Whatever their differences, they could work them out in and out of bed.

Hunter moved his hips, nudging and withdrawing until her body accepted his invasion. His jaw clenched as his pace quickened, but his thrusts deepened until one thrust stretched her maidenhead and allowed him to fill her completely.

Although he had attempted not to hurt her, Grace's eyes widened and she gasped as his pelvis met hers.

"Am I hurting you?"

She shook her head. "Not precisely," she replied, her voice sounding as strained as his.

It was all Hunter needed to hear. Drawing in a deep breath, he kissed her on the lips. It was a tender apology for hurting her, even though he could not bring himself to regret it.

He withdrew slowly, testing her resolve as well as his own. If she had begged him to stop, he did not know if he had the strength to heed her command. He had figured out from their first meeting that Grace was hell on his good intentions.

She smiled up at him, her expression full of wonderment and innocence. Never had seduction felt so right. Hunter grinned down at her and then began to move in earnest. He heard her soft gasp, but he did not slow his pace. His right hand slid down her side and cupped the soft curve of her buttock.

Hunter thrust fully into her womanly sheath, using his grip to deepen his penetration. Grace moaned, her hands wandering as she explored the flesh within her reach.

He would never survive, if she ever got her hands on his cock.

"You are so wicked," she murmured against his mouth.

Hunter took advantage of her exposed throat and tasted the salt of her flesh as it glistened and glided against his body, which was slick with his exertions and restraint.

He was so caught up in relishing her responses that some of the rigid control he had always prided himself on slipped. His thrusts had slowed in tempo, but were forceful and deep. His testicles slapped against her bottom with each delicious thrust.

Grace's gaze was unfocused as she delighted in his wild claiming. Then she dug her nails into his sides and cried out, her body shuddering as the pleasure washed over her. She was not alone. Hunter tensed, his teeth snapping together as he could no longer resist the siren call of her body. His hot, virile seed burst forth, and he groaned at the exquisite agony of pumping himself into the woman who had tormented him from the very beginning.

Hunter shuddered, drawing her tightly against him. The crazed lust was easing, but the longing had yet to diminish. "Grace?"

"Yes," she replied, sounding bemused and out of breath.

"Can you take me again?"

His cock twitched within her, and she laughed.

"Are you ever satisfied?"

"Ah, a challenge," he murmured, kissing her while he indulged himself by filling his hand with her breast. "Have I mentioned how much I enjoy challenges?"

For the first time, Hunter had no desire to slip away from his lover's bed.

Grace awoke uncertain what had disturbed her sleep. She rolled over and sighed, realizing that she was alone in the bed.

Hunter had sought his own bed.

She had no right to be disappointed, but she was. Before he had fallen asleep, he had told her that he was staying. She was supposed to awaken in her husband's arms.

Perhaps it was one promise Hunter was incapable of keeping.

Grace sat up and winced. She was sore, but it was to be expected. Her husband, she discovered, possessed an insatiable appetite. He had reached for her three times during the long night of lovemaking. She wondered if the last time truly counted because she had been half asleep when he had taken her.

Thankfully, her body had not disappointed her. It had recognized Hunter's touch, allowing him to claim her with little coaxing. She shivered and blindly reached for her nightgown.

If her husband was incapable of sleeping in her bed, perhaps she could slip into his. Grace pulled the nightgown over her head and walked to the door.

When she opened it, she gasped. Immediately, she began coughing.

Now she knew what had awakened her.

The heavy scent of smoke.

The house was on fire.

"Hunter!"

Hunter awoke facedown on the marble floor. What was he doing in the front hall? Had he been drinking? His head hurt, which confirmed that too much brandy might be the culprit.

Grace.

His memories returned like a flash of lightning. He had not been drinking. He had been shagging his wife in her bedchamber. Numerous times. Why had he left her warm bed?

He had promised to stay.

"Hunter!"

His head lifted sharply at the sound of his name, and he groaned. He tried to touch his head, and that was when he realized that his wrists were bound behind his back.

"Grace?" he called out, and grimaced at how weak he sounded. He coughed a few times. His throat felt raw. He turned his head to the side and noticed the smoke billowing from the corridor that led to the kitchen. He squinted at the smoke and saw the eerie glow that indicated one thing.

There was a fire.

"Good, you have awakened." The familiar voice

had him turning his head to confront the intruder. "I had despaired that I might have hit you too hard. My goal was not murder, but to addle you so I could restrain you."

"Christ, Walker, if this is some sort of jest," he snarled, struggling against his bindings. Overhead, he heard Grace call out his name.

His cousin crouched down in front of him. "It is no jest, Hunter. In fact, I am deadly earnest in my desire for your demise."

Hunter lowered his head until his forehead rested on the cool marble. "It wasn't Strangham. Grace was never the target. It was me. You shot at me when we stopped along the road."

Walker seized him by the hair and pulled up his head so their gazes met. "It was truly brilliant on my part. I knew you had your suspicions about Strangham. After all, the man had stood by as his brother died, and then he proceeded to poison the widow when she told him that she was possibly breeding the duke's heir. Can you believe it? What rotten luck, I say."

He twisted his head free from his cousin's merciless grasp, and turned his head to the side to cough. "Considering the murderer possesses the title and still lives, he has done fairly well."

"Not as well as one might believe, my dear cousin. Regretfully, Strangham has perished from a regrettable accident."

"Did you murder him?" Hunter rasped, attempting to keep his cousin distracted. He tugged on the ropes at his wrists. They held, but he had an incentive to keep trying.

"Let's just say that I helped him along. He was a despicable man. No appreciation for his good fortune or the title."

"And you showed him the error of his ways."

If he could just keep his cousin talking, he might be able to escape the ropes.

"Enough! Do you think I am a fool, Hunter?" He stood and slowly turned, his gesture intended to encompass the entire hall. "You hope to distract me. Perhaps even talk me out of my murderous intent."

"Why would I do that, cousin?" A bout of coughing prevented him from continuing. "You clearly have developed a taste for killing."

"Not just killing," he admitted. "I have other vices, too. Not that you appeared to appreciate my skills. Do you recall the time I worked up the nerve to ask you if I might become of a member of Nox?"

"I told you to forget it, but I never told you the real reason why." Hunter grinned up at him. "Shall I tell you? It was because you were unworthy. All of us laughed at the notion of inviting you."

Walker retaliated by delivering a ruthless kick to Hunter's left side.

"Gah!" Christ, he hurt. His cousin might have broken a rib or two with that kick. "Is that all you've got? The dowager kicked harder than you."

It was difficult to ignore the fire licking up the

walls, but Hunter had more pressing problems. This time when his cousin attacked, Hunter rolled onto his side and brought his legs together in a scissor motion.

"No!" his cousin screamed as he landed on his arse.

Hunter kicked at him again, but the man simply rolled out of reach.

Damn!

Prepared for his tricks, Walker avoided Hunter's next attack and managed to deliver three more hard kicks to his cousin's bruised side.

"Bastard," Hunter hissed and spat. There was blood mixed in with his spittle. "It's me that you are angry with. Let Grace go."

Walker groaned in frustration. "Were you not listening about Strangham? The mother was breeding an heir. That's why she had to die." He pointed heavenward. "If you had managed to keep your hands off her, I might have allowed her to live. But I know what you were doing upstairs in her bedchamber. I'll wager you could not resist spilling your seed in her. After all, she has to deliver your heir in eighteen months."

If Hunter had resisted Grace one more day, he might have spared her a grisly death by fire. Coughing, he curled into a ball and tried to think past the pain. If he didn't think of something, Grace was going to die.

"Walker, you have no desire to hang for Strangham's murder." He swallowed and tried to clear his throat. "Perhaps we can negotiate new terms. I married Grace, but I am willing to give you the dowager's inheritance. It's yours."

"Why should I settle for just a stipend when I can have the title, too?" Walker braced his hands on his knees. "I will regret killing Grace. She's a beautiful woman. As you smother and burn on your marble flooring, I want you to lie here knowing that I will be the last man to fuck her before she dies."

"Leave her alone!" Hunter roared, which was ruined by another coughing fit.

"There's nothing you can do to stop me."

"Perhaps not, but I might have something to say about it," Grace said, swinging her weapon with all her might. The copper bedpan connected with Walker's temple, and he dropped like a stone. "A very nice lady once told me that a bedpan was a highly effective weapon when dealing with querulous husbands. It apparently works on murderers, too."

"Duly noted," Hunter said dully, fighting to remain conscious. "Did you manage to kill him?"

Grace dropped the bedpan and picked up a large vase that was once treasured by his grandmother. "Not quite. But I am not convinced the bedpan has done its job. He might be feigning his injuries."

With that she brought the vase down on the crazy fool's head. It shattered on impact.

Walker did not move.

"Did you cut yourself?"

Grace frowned as she stared at her hands. "Not a scratch."

"Good. Now pick up one of those shards of pottery and cut me free," he said, his voice strengthening as his concern for their lives increased and the flames climbed. "You did notice the house is on fire."

"It is kind of you to point that out, my love," Grace said as she sawed her way through Hunter's bindings.

When he was free, he grabbed her wrist. "Am I? Your love, that is."

"Of course, you daft man. I fell in love with your miniature years before I met you in the flesh." Her gaze shifted to his cousin. "I suppose we have to save him."

"Aye. Newgate prefers living prisoners," Hunter said, getting onto his feet without his wife's assistance. "And one more thing, Duchess."

"Yes?"

"I love you," he said, his declaration bringing tears to her eyes. "I didn't marry you out of duty. I married you because I realized that I have always belonged to you, ever since that first day when you set your sharp baby teeth into my wrist. I am so damn sorry that I fought it so long."

"Do not fret," She covered her mouth and coughed. "I am certain I can think of a way you can make it up to me."

Someone broke down the front door.

Belatedly, Hunter noticed that Walker must have barred all of the main doors to prevent anyone from entering or leaving the burning house. As men rushed into the hall to rescue the sleeping inhabitants, Hunter took Grace's hand. Together they strolled out through the destroyed front door, joyful in the knowledge that they had saved the one thing that was priceless to each of them.

Don't miss these other Lords of Vice novels by
ALEXANDRA HAWKINS

ALL AFTERNOON WITH A
SCANDALOUS MARQUESS

SUNRISE WITH A NOTORIOUS LORD

AFTER DARK WITH A SCOUNDREL

TILL DAWN WITH THE DEVIL

ALL NIGHT WITH A ROGUE

Available from St. Martin's Paperbacks